'Spend time with me,' he murmured.

'If you're so sure we're incompatible, prove it to me. Anywhere. Any time. Pick somewhere you'll feel safe.'

'And would I be?' Susan twisted her head, lifting her shoulder to force his mouth away, his breath too disturbing against her ear. Adam hadn't kissed her and held her lightly, barely touching her, but she seemed to be shivering uncontrollably. 'Would I be safe?'

He was still for a few seconds. 'Sure you want to be?'

A New Zealand doctor with restless feet, **Helen Shelton** has lived and worked in Britain, and travelled widely. Married to an Australian she met while on safari in Africa, she recently moved to Sydney, where they plan to settle for a little while at least. She has always been an enthusiastic reader and writer, and inspiration for the background for her medical romances comes directly from her own experiences working in hospitals in several countries around the world.

Recent titles by the same author:

AN UNGUARDED MOMENT
ONE MAGICAL KISS
CONTRACT DAD
A MATTER OF PRACTICE
A SURGEON'S SEARCH
POPPY'S PASSION

A SURGEON
FOR SUSAN

BY
HELEN SHELTON

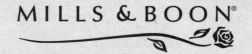

MILLS & BOON®

All the characters in this book have no existence outside the imagination of the author, and have no relation whatsoever to anyone bearing the same name or names. They are not even distantly inspired by any individual known or unknown to the author, and all the incidents are pure invention.

First published in Great Britain 1999
Harlequin Mills & Boon Limited,
Eton House, 18-24 Paradise Road, Richmond, Surrey TW9 1SR

© Poppytech Services Ltd 1999

ISBN 0 263 81718 0

Set in Times Roman 10½ on 12 pt.
03-9907-51243-D

Printed and bound in Spain
by Litografía Rosés, S.A., Barcelona

CHAPTER ONE

'AN ORTHOPAEDIC surgeon?' Susan stared at her younger sister, appalled. 'Annabel, you're mad. You've come all this way, insisted on seeing me, dragged me out of an interview and interrupted my schedule just to tell me about some lonely orthopaedic surgeon?'

'He's six feet one,' Annabel continued irritatingly. 'And it wasn't an important interview. Your secretary told me it was just a drug rep, hawking freebies, and we all know how much you hate that. Now...' her eyes went down again to study the newsletter she held '...he's got dark hair and green eyes. He's a Scorpio—'

'I don't care about his star sign.' Susan groaned. 'An orthopaedic surgeon? Absolutely and for ever no. Don't do this to me, Annie. I know you think you're helping me but, I promise you, you're wrong. You've chosen the wrong man. It would never work. Not in a million years.'

'Why in the world would anybody be biased against orthopaedic surgeons?'

Susan hesitated. 'They're not very bright,' she informed her sister finally, being as delicate as she could while still conveying the message honestly. 'Men of action but intellectual...fleas. And I'm not biased. It's a fact.'

'Scorpio's perfect for you,' Annabel continued determinedly, the faint narrowing of her perfectly made-up eyes the only sign that she realised that Susan wasn't taking this as breathtakingly gratefully as she'd probably anticipated she would. 'Perhaps not as perfect as a Capricorn, but still perfect.'

Susan took a deep breath. 'Get lost.'

'For goodness' sake, Susan!' Annabel actually looked cross. 'For once in your dull, dull, horrible life listen to someone other than one of your precious patients! You're turning into an old prune. This is for your own good.'

Startled at hearing such confrontational language from her normally more subtly manipulative sister, Susan's mouth dropped open, and the younger woman looked pointedly back at the advertisement she was reading.

'He's thirty-six. He owns his own home—'

'I'm not an old prune.'

'No, just heading that way at the speed of light.'

'My life isn't dull.'

'Oh, yes, it is.' Annabel clicked her tongue. 'Dull, dreary and boring. Work, work, work—that's you. Just how many other thirty-four-year-old virgins do you think there are walking around in this world?'

'Quite a few, I would imagine.' Hurt firstly by the description of her life—a life which Susan herself found quite pleasant, if a little predictable—and secondly that Annabel could take such a personal and difficult-to-reveal confidence and throw it back in her face the way she'd just done, Susan drew herself up stiffly. 'Religious people, and people saving themselves because they want to make a very special commitment to someone they love.'

'And old prunes,' her sister added, 'who aren't particularly religious at all but just never go out with any men so they never get the opportunity not to save themselves.'

'I go out.'

'Dreary lectures with Dr Dullby Dingbat don't count.'

'*Duncan Dilly,*' Susan said sharply.

'Whoever.' Annabel rolled her eyes. 'The man's a fossil.'

'Duncan's a very nice man. He's a scholar and a gifted

psychiatrist,' Susan pronounced loyally. 'I'm very fond of him.'

'Fond?' Annabel screwed up her face. 'Out with Dullby,' she ordered unceremoniously. 'I've seen more life in a dog bone.'

'Conveniently bringing us back to the subject of your orthopaedic surgeon,' Susan pointed out unhappily. 'Orthopaedic surgeons are the Neanderthals of the medical profession,' she explained. 'I'm sorry, I feel terrible about insulting a whole speciality but all doctors know it's true. A dog bone has more brains than an orthopaedic surgeon. Not to mention more wit, better conversation and more advanced social skills. Forget it, Annabel. Please, please, just forget it.'

'Susie, you can't spend the rest of your life alone.'

'I'm not...opposed to meeting someone interesting,' Susan admitted reluctantly, guessing from Annabel's triumphant beam that there'd be no deflecting her sister now on this. 'And you're right about me hardly ever meeting anyone and, all right, sometimes, occasionally, I do get a little lonely.' Like increasingly these days late at night when she dragged herself away from work and back to her empty little flat. More and more as around her her friends married and started families. 'But this man is totally unsuitable,' she insisted, positive at least about that. 'Find me someone I have something in common with so at least we can hold a decent conversation and I'll reconsider.'

'First let me finish this one,' her sister said firmly. 'Where was I...? Right, so he's thirty-six and he owns his own home. He's never been married—'

'Gay,' Susan supplied, perking up.

'There's a separate column for that and...he's not in it,' Annabel said crisply, checking. 'He likes blondes and brunettes and redheads,' she read, more loudly now, as if she thought that might drown out the derisive sound Susan emitted. 'And his hobbies are sailing, squash, scuba-diving, climbing and rugby.'

'You're right. We're perfectly suited,' Susan observed. 'Given that my hobbies are reading, knitting, watching television and embroidery, I can see that we'd just get on magnificently.'

'You can't embroider, you don't own a television and the only thing you've ever knitted is a peggy square full of holes—and that was twenty-five years ago,' Annabel snapped. 'You have no hobbies because you can't keep away from your dreary work for five minutes and person-ally I think that's pitiful. Pull yourself together, Susan. Show some appreciation. I've put a lot of effort into this.'

'What effort?' Susan went blank. 'Bringing this clipping in to show me, you mean?'

'If you check the date you'll notice that this was pub-lished almost three weeks ago,' Annabel announced with what in other circumstances might have been interpreted as pride. 'In the meantime, I've been extremely busy. *You*, Susan, believe it or not, are meeting this gorgeous man tonight, outside Covent Garden tube at eight. Now let me read the rest of it.'

While Susan lapsed into shocked, appalled silence, her sister continued happily, '"Looking for sincere relation-ship with warm, loving, sensitive woman. View: long term and marriage." There.' She beamed. 'What did I tell you? Doesn't it sound wonderful? His picture's not bad either.' She fished around in a voluminous handbag and produced a snapshot. 'What do you think?'

Susan took the blurred photograph automatically. Taken from a beach, it showed an athletic-looking, dark-haired man, riding a sailboard. 'First time I've ever seen an or-thopod wearing anything other than a blue blazer with gold buttons,' she murmured, acknowledging inwardly that he certainly possessed above-average good looks.

'But I'm not interested,' she insisted. She was already confident they were incompatible and the photograph merely reinforced her certainty.

Her—albeit limited—experience of men had taught her, firstly, that she was immune to sex appeal and, secondly, that going out with someone with whom she shared no common interests invariably signalled an embarrassing evening of stilted conversation with the risk of an igno-minious struggle to extract herself from an enthusiastic embrace at the end of it.

Plus—she studied the surgeon's photo without plea-sure—she'd discovered that better-looking men tended to be more insistent in their attempts to persuade her into their beds. Which meant—since she hadn't yet found any man's embrace anything other than embarrassing and awk-ward—that she preferred the less physically perfect ex-amples of the sex.

Being single wasn't something that worried Susan her-self too much yet. She loved her work and for now, aside from those occasional moments of loneliness, psychiatry fulfilled her. But sensibly, she thought in an understated way, she was aware of the passing of time. Since she did nurture hopes of one day having children she knew she should be making more of an effort to expand her social life in the hope of meeting someone special.

It was that awareness of time passing which had pre-vented her stopping Annabel from taking her on as her latest project and it was that same awareness now which told her that it was important not to waste time meeting men who were clearly unsuitable. Men like this ortho-paedic surgeon.

She wouldn't let Annabel bully her into a date and she

wasn't going to mope about feeling sorry for him for having to advertise in a lonely hearts column because with his looks he was bound to be deluged with enough other offers to soothe his ego for life.

She took a deep breath. 'Annabel, I really don't think—'

'Sexy, I think.' Annabel, beside her, was studying the picture with an intensity that Susan found just a little distasteful. 'Look at those thighs. Wow. And that chest. I wouldn't mind snuggling up to that for a few hours on a gloomy winter afternoon.'

She saw Susan's disgusted expression and let out a giggle. 'All right, all right. If I wasn't already happily married,' she amended finally. 'You're such a prude, Susie. A pruney prude. Loosen up before it's too late and no one wants you.'

Determined not to let that comment worry her, Susan passed the photograph back to her sister. 'Please call him and cancel whatever ridiculous arrangements you've made.'

'I don't have his number,' Annabel said blithely.

'That's what directory assistance is for.'

'I don't know his last name.'

'Annabel!'

'His *pen* name is Adam,' Annabel explained brightly, clearly still determined to ignore Susan's protests. 'As in Adam and Eve, I imagine. I expect you'll exchange real names tonight. He'll be carrying a black brolley and holding an *Evening Standard*.'

'Like every other man in London at this time of year,' Susan observed, exasperated now. It was late, late autumn, almost December, and it had been raining most of the past week. 'Annie, you're hopeless. Hopeless and mad. I'm not going to meet him.'

'But it's all arranged.'

'Well, you go. Explain that it's all been a mistake and say sorry and just…wish him well or something.'

'Susan, you can't do this to me.' For the first time, Susan saw that she'd managed to genuinely alarm her sister. 'And I can't. Not tonight. Mike and I are going to parents' night at Em's school.'

'So the surgeon gets stood up.' Susan felt a pang of guilt at that but she struggled not to let it bother her, reminding herself again that men who looked the way he did couldn't possibly be without admirers.

'You can't!' Annabel looked shocked. 'That's awful. The poor man. Imagine how he'll feel.'

'He's an orthopod,' Susan reminded her. 'He'll have quite a thick skin.'

'But what if he doesn't?'

'Annie, stop it,' Susan protested, determined—absolutely determined—not to be pushed into this. 'Believe me, I trained with doctors who went on to become orthopaedic surgeons. They're not like you and me. They don't have the same sorts of feelings. He'll be like a frog's leg. He'll react by reflex. If no one's there he'll just shrug and go off for a beer with his friends. We don't have to worry about him.'

Annabel picked up the advertisement again. '"Looking for sincere relationship with warm, loving, sensitive woman. View: long term and marriage"', she repeated. 'Since when did a frog's leg write something as wonderful as that?'

Susan had to admit that the gentle, careful words weren't the usual sort of outpourings she'd have expected from an orthopod. A psychiatrist like herself, certainly, a physician, yes, perhaps even a paediatrician, but never, never an orthopaedic surgeon.

'Please, don't,' she said unhappily, as it occurred to her

that the poor man might possibly be an outcast among his own kind. And if he was such a sensitive soul in such a profession then he was no doubt used to having his feelings heavily trampled by his unfailingly macho colleagues. 'Don't,' she said again, less firmly this time. 'You're just trying to make me feel guilty.'

'"Sincere relationship",' Annabel read again. '"Warm, loving, sensitive woman".'

'Stop it.'

'"View: long term and marriage."'

'Meeting him would be a complete waste of time for both of us.'

'Just imagine him.' Annabel sighed dramatically. 'The poor man. Will he wait till nine, do you think? Or will he stay till midnight?'

'Annabel—'

'At first he'll think it's the trains,' she continued, her eyes avoiding her sister's as she carried on over Susan's protest. 'He'll think you've been held up. So he'll wait for a few more trains to come through, half a dozen I suppose. And then...then he'll start to get worried. He might think there's been a bomb scare or an accident. He won't want to go down to the platform to check if the trains are still coming because then he might miss you in the lift if you've just arrived. So he'll try the ticket office first. He'll ask—'

'All right, all right, I'll meet him,' Susan moaned finally. 'Just once. Just tonight. But only if you stop now. Stop before you make me weep.'

Annabel looked as though she wasn't sure whether or not to trust her. 'Promise?'

'Promise.'

'Solemn promise?'

'Solemn promise,' Susan said wearily. 'Eight o'clock. Covent Garden tube. Black umbrella. *Evening Standard*.'

'You'll have a wonderful time.' Annabel hugged her and Susan found herself briefly enveloped in the expensive, heady fragrance of her sister's latest favourite perfume. 'I just know tonight will be fantastic for you. He's perfect. You're perfect for each other.'

'Wrong.' Susan drew back sharply from Annabel's embrace. 'It'll be miserable,' she said wearily. 'We'll have nothing in common and nothing to talk about, but all I'm going to do is meet him and explain that it's all been some horrible mistake. At least then I won't be sitting here unable to concentrate on my reports because I feel too guilty.'

'You'll see I'm right.' Moving quickly now, Annabel collected her things together. 'Good,' she said smartly. 'I have to dash. I'll call you in the morning. I want to hear every little detail.'

'Wait.' Susan followed her to the door of her office then through her secretary's, relieved that Rachel didn't seem to be about. 'Annabel, you said something before about using pen names. What's mine?'

'Sex Kitten. Your name is Sex Kitten.'

Susan took an involuntary, horrified breath, but Annabel, backing away now along the corridor towards the lifts, just smiled smugly at her.

'Close your mouth before you catch a fly. Be reasonable, Susie. With an advertisement like his he probably had hundreds of replies. I had to get his attention somehow.'

'Sex Kitten?' Susan stared at her, appalled as much by the words themselves as the utter irony of such a title being applied to someone like her. She looked around quickly, checking that there was no one about to overhear them. *'Sex Kitten?'*

'I thought it had a nice ring to it.' Annabel held out a defensive arm as if to fend her off even though Susan hadn't moved from the doorway. 'It certainly did the trick,' she added brightly. 'In his letter he sounded keen. Very keen.'

'Where's the letter?'

'I left it at home.'

'What did it say?'

'Just how much he was looking forward to meeting you,' she said blandly. 'And how much he liked your photo.'

Susan froze. 'What photo?'

'A holiday snap.'

'Which holiday snap?'

But the lift doors behind Annabel chimed, then opened. Before Susan could stop her, Annabel gave her a little encouraging wave and darted in and away from her.

Susan started after her but, realising that there was no way she'd get down three flights of stairs and through the fire doors in time to catch Annabel if her sister was determined to escape, she gave up after a few steps and stomped back to her office.

She swore, then slammed her door. Both were things she rarely if ever did but she felt as if the circumstances warranted some form of violent response.

'Cervical spine, normal alignment, no fractures,' Adam said slowly, working through each of his new patient's X-rays and CT scans in turn. 'No skull fracture. Radiological rib fractures right ninth through eleventh, chest drain *in situ*. Small right fluid collection. Scapula, shoulder, clavicle bilaterally and sternum normal. Transverse fracture right upper humerus, minimal displacement. Upper limbs otherwise normal. T and L spines normal on limited view. Complete disruption pelvic rim anteriorly and posteriorly with displacement of right sacroiliac joint and pubic symphysis. Any evidence of organ damage?'

'Retrograde urethrogram and cystogram show bladder and urethra intact,' his registrar said crisply, pushing up the pictures so he could confirm that. 'No problems catheterising him. No evidence of abdominal or neural damage at this stage.'

Adam nodded. He moved onto the next films. 'Midshaft transverse fracture left femur, distal transverse fracture right femur, patellae, tibs and fibs look OK. What was it? RTA?'

'Motorcycle versus lorry,' his registrar elaborated, coming with him to Tony Dundas's bed where Adam started to examine him. 'He was thrown twenty yards and landed on his right side.'

Adam carefully palpated their unconscious patient's abdomen. 'And otherwise?'

'CT shows no intracranial bleed, small right haemothorax, chest drain in place, as you've noted. Negative abdominal tap for blood so the general surgeons aren't interested.' Lawrence Noble, the anaesthetist in co-charge with Adam of London's St Martin's Hospital's trauma unit, spoke promptly.

'Good.' Adam nodded again, pleased. Swiftly he completed the rest of his checks, then straightened. 'Then he's all ours,' he declared. 'We'll get on and get his pelvis stabilised and the rest of his bones nailed. Chris, what's happening?'

'Theatre's ready as soon as we are,' his registrar said quickly. 'We haven't been able to get a relative in to organise the consent but his father has faxed us his permission and Administration's OK'd that.'

'Then let's move.' It was just after three in the afternoon, a rare time for theatre space to appear, and he wanted to take advantage of it. By starting now, they'd be through soon after six when the general and gynae surgeons on call for the evening would be queuing up to start their own emergency work.

'Adam, a private word before you go…?'

'Larry, I've told you I'm not interested.' As well as being a colleague, Lawrence Noble was his brother-in-law and now Adam slapped the X-rays down onto the trolley and sent him an impatient look. 'Forget it.'

'But she's expecting you,' Lawrence protested. 'Barbara's organised everything. Covent Garden tube. Eight o'clock. You can't back out now.'

'I'm not backing out,' Adam pointed out tersely, inclining his head to indicate that his registrar should go on ahead of him to Theatres. 'I'm not backing out,' he repeated, 'because I never agreed to meet the woman in the first place. I never agreed to any of this. I don't care how wonderful you both think she sounds, Larry. I'm too busy—'

'Adam, I'm stuck in the middle here,' Lawrence interjected. 'Give me a break on this. I know where you're coming from but I've got Barbara in my other ear full time about tonight. If I go home and tell her you're standing this woman up she'll kill me. She's organised everything. And you know you agreed, by omission if not by consent. You've known for months what she was up to and you just let her go on.'

'She won't kill you,' Adam growled. 'For reasons that continue to escape me, Babs actually appears quite fond of you. And the only reason I didn't stop her was because I thought it'd keep her quiet for five minutes. Against someone like your wife, any sane man would have done the same thing. It doesn't mean I'm interested. It never occurred to me that she'd go so far as to actually select some poor woman.'

'Come on, you'll get on great.' But the anaesthetist looked worried. 'She's a doctor.'

Adam frowned. 'What sort of doctor?'

'Well…a psychiatrist,' the other man said slowly, grimacing at Adam's dark look. 'All right, all right,' he conceded lamely. 'Point taken. But, remember, a psychiatrist still has a medical degree. In every other way I swear she's you.'

'Larry—'

A polite cough from the trauma unit's charge nurse brought Adam's head back sharply. 'Adam, sorry to interrupt.' Margaret's twinkling regard suggested she'd overheard at least some of their discussion. 'Would you just sign this, please?' She passed him a form pinned to the front of a set of notes. 'It's the request for Mr Wilson's outpatient orthotics referral. Administration's decided that all referrals must come directly from the consultants now. And personally I think the blind date with the psychiatrist sounds like a fantastic idea.'

'Thanks.' Adam lifted his eyes to the ceiling, before scrawling his name along the line the nurse had indicated. 'For nothing,' he added. 'What's your angle?'

'Purely a selfish one,' Margaret said easily. 'I'm sick to death of watching all my nurses turning gaga when you're around. Getting you married off won't stop it but it might take the edge off—and the sooner the better, as far as I'm concerned.'

'Gaga?' Lawrence looked interested. 'I didn't know that. I suppose that's how they used to be about me as well before Barbara snapped me up.'

'No, Larry, no.' Margaret patted his arm kindly. 'Sorry, but no.'

'So it's just in the looks, is it?' The anaesthetist looked disappointed. 'He's dark and strong and I'm just pale and sickly, am I? I'll have you know, Margaret, that underneath these *ordinary* features and this thick jumper I'm as sexy as Adam. He hasn't got anything that I haven't.'

'I believe you.' Margaret's amused gaze met Adam's exasperated one. 'And we love you, Lawrence. We might not lust after your body quite the way we do after Adam's, but we still love you. Be happy with that.'

'What do you think she means?' Lawrence mused, once the nurse had gone off back to the ward again. 'Do you think she's patronising me?'

'Everyone patronises you, Larry,' Adam observed dryly. He checked his watch. It was ten minutes since the theatre porters had taken their patient past them towards Theatres. 'Now, forget tonight,' he said flatly, turning away. 'I've got to get downstairs—'

'I'll come with you,' the anaesthetist insisted, trotting after him along the corridor. 'Adam, listen to me. You think I'm joking about Barbara killing me? I'm not. If you don't go tonight I'm dead. I can't believe she hasn't tried getting hold of you herself.'

'If trying to get hold of me means leaving eighteen urgent messages with my secretary then I suppose she's been trying,' Adam conceded. Wary of his sister in the determined mood she appeared to be in, he'd made no attempt to reply to any of them.

'Eighteen?' Lawrence whistled. 'I really am in trouble. Adam—'

'No.'

'One night—'

'I'm busy, Larry.' He took the stairs two at a time. 'I

won't finish this case before six and I've two weeks' worth of data to go through in the lab tonight.'

'All right, you're forcing me to do this,' the other man said cryptically. 'Stop, Adam. You know they won't be ready for you yet. Just give me two minutes.'

Conceding that Lawrence was right, at least about the theatre staff not being ready for him immediately, Adam drew up. 'Two minutes,' he agreed tersely. 'Go.'

'I promised Barbara I wasn't going to show you this unless I was desperate,' the other man said hastily, 'but, man to man, I know that it's the only thing that's going to reach you.' With an air akin to that of a magician pulling off one of his best tricks he produced a photograph from the top pocket of his white coat. He passed it to Adam. 'This is her.' He waited a few seconds. 'What do you think?'

'Nice,' Adam admitted reluctantly, granting the curvaceous breasts the leisurely appraisal they certainly deserved. 'Very nice.' Photographed on a beach, the dark-haired woman was lying back under an umbrella, her eyes closed, long hair forming a halo around her face, arms stretched provocatively above her head. Part of an unfastened bikini top was visible beneath her as if she'd rolled over and dislodged it, leaving her pale, beautifully formed body bare apart from a tiny triangle of pink between her hips. 'All right, I'm finding myself a little more enthusiastic,' he admitted, his eyes narrowing. 'What's the story?'

'She describes herself as a "sexy, fun-loving, romantic woman looking for enthusiastic, energetic, *passionate* life experiences",' Lawrence recounted, referring to a note he'd retrieved from his opposite pocket.

More interested now than he was ready to admit, Adam noted the fragrant scent drifting from the letter Lawrence held.

Workwise, Adam had been more than fully committed this past year. The retirement of his closest senior colleague and the administration's determination not to replace the surgeon with a new appointment meant that his own clinic and ward load had increased dramatically. His research had to come after that. Since the few spare hours he did manage to scratch together tended to be devoted to keeping himself in a reasonable state of fitness, his social life, invariably his last priority, had been neglected.

But now, admiring the exquisite shape of the angel in the picture Lawrence had passed him, he was reminded of just how many months it was since he'd spent time with a woman. For the first time in a long time he found himself tempted. The fact that meeting her wasn't going to take any of his own effort to set up made the idea even more attractive.

'I'll do it,' he said finally, aware of Lawrence hovering impatiently beside him. 'But that doesn't mean that I think this whole scheme of Barbara's is anything other than insane.'

'She just wants to see you married off and happy.' Lawrence's relief was obvious from the width of his grin. 'So this is…what? What shall I tell her? That you're actually interested now or that you're only committing yourself to one night away from work?'

'One night,' Adam decreed. 'There're some statistics to collate but the paper we're doing now is practically finished. I can afford a break.'

'She writes that she's "a reluctant Virgo, *in every sense of the word*".' Lawrence had looked down at the letter he still clutched and now he shrugged and looked back up at Adam. 'I don't know what that means. Barbara was a little bit worried about it but she's decided that it probably just means she's a perfectionist. She prefers indoor sports but she's "willing to try anything once".' He whistled softly. 'Sounds pretty good to me,' he said thickly.

'Unfortunately for you you're married to my sister,' Adam pointed out dryly. 'And Babs *would* kill you if she caught you looking, let alone trying anything. Give me that.'

He tugged the scented note out of his brother-in-law's hand. '"Looking for a fun, loving relationship",' he read. '"View: let's see what happens".' He blinked at the signature. '"Sex Kitten"? Sex Kitten!'

'It's a pen name,' Lawrence told him quickly. 'It's normal to use one in these circumstances.'

Adam sent him a narrowed look. 'You seem to know a lot about it.'

'Barbara explained.' The anaesthetist shrugged again. 'She knows all about the protocol of these advertisements. The one she wrote for you was terrific.'

'Show me.'

'I haven't got it.'

But Lawrence looked shifty, Adam decided, and he tensed. 'What did it say?'

'Just a basic description. Height, hair colour, age, hobbies, the usual.'

'That's all?'

'Virtually all.' Seeming marginally more confident, the other man rushed on, 'There've been hundreds of replies but this is the best one and Sex Kitten's the prettiest by far. Barbara wasn't that keen on her at first because she thought that the whole package was too over the top, but I knew you'd be interested.'

Adam sent him a hard look, knowing, after seeing the note and the photograph, exactly what Barbara had meant, but Lawrence seemed unperturbed now.

'My argument was that, besides being gorgeous, this

one's a doctor. That immediately means you've got something to talk about.'

'She's a psychiatrist,' Adam reminded him.

'Still a doctor,' Lawrence insisted. 'Anyway, knowing your luck you won't be doing much talking.'

Adam frowned. 'Larry, that's not—'

'Eight o'clock.' Apparently realising that Adam was having second thoughts, and determined not to give him any opportunity to voice them, Lawrence swivelled on the stairs. 'Covent Garden tube. Black umbrella. *Evening Standard*. She'll be waiting. Promise you'll tell me all about it tomorrow.'

He winced at the dark look Adam gave him in reply to that. 'Just don't forget that I'm anaesthetising for you tomorrow morning. Want me to put a bleep out for you in the morning?'

'I'll make it.' Adam waved him away impatiently. He hadn't yet met a woman who could keep him away from his work and, despite this one's obvious attractions, he didn't see any reason to think she'd prove any different.

CHAPTER TWO

SUSAN was late getting to Covent Garden tube station. Although nervous and cross and embarrassed all at once, overwhelmingly she was conscious of being wet. The downpour which had been threatening all afternoon had hit fast and hard at the precise moment her bus had dropped her in Charing Cross Road.

In her nervousness about the evening she'd left her raincoat in her office, but unexpectedly heavy traffic on the bus trip into the West End meant that she was running too late to take shelter.

Now, although the rain had eased to a feeble drizzle, she still felt like a waterlogged sponge. Miserably aware that her sodden hair was caked to her face and scalp, that her face had to be as red and blotchy as it was damp from the effort of hurrying and that her spectacles were smeared and misted, she muttered a few subdued apologies and squeezed into the crowd sheltering under the roof of the tube station.

Undoing her jacket, she wiped her glasses on the skirt of her suit, about the only part of her that was dry since the water had managed to soak through the neckline of her jacket and into her blouse. Once she could see again she ventured out of the shelter, intent on finding the orthopod, but despite the lessening of the force of the shower the roads still ran with water and a passing cab managed to spray her shoulder-high with water, leaving her dripping again.

Her apologies even more feeble this time, Susan wiggled

back into the crowd, brushing self-consciously at her skirt and jacket in a pathetic attempt to shed some of the moisture. Vowing to strangle Annabel at the earliest opportunity, she decided that the least uncomfortable course was to stay put and let the surgeon find her on the strength of whichever holiday snap Annabel had seen fit to send him.

Besides, the odds of her finding him amongst the crowd had to be extremely low, she told herself firmly, doing her best to pretend that she wasn't trying to find a loophole in her agreement to meet the man. The picture of him on the sailboard hadn't been clear enough for her to recognise him easily and the corners around the tube station were packed with people who all seemed to be waiting for other people. Virtually everyone, she noted wearily, bore damp, black umbrellas and *Evening Standard*s.

It took her a little while to realise that a couple standing across the road in the shelter of some sort of knick-knack store were watching her. The stocky-looking man in the heavy coat and Wellington boots was too short to be Adam Sailboarder because the orthopod had written that he was over six feet tall, but he still—definitely—seemed to be staring at her. She couldn't see the man's face because, like his companion, he wore a baseball cap pulled down over his face and heavy black sunglasses.

Odd, she decided, considering it was virtually winter and London hadn't seen sunshine in two weeks. Also it had been dark for ages.

Both of them looked away quite sharply when she stared back at them.

Experimentally she turned a little, pretending not to be looking at them, but when she turned back quickly she captured them watching her again. The woman looked down, as if embarrassed about studying her, and the man turned right around and peered intently into the shop.

Susan told herself that she was getting paranoid. To distract herself, she made a half-hearted effort to inspect the crowd. Working her way from the couple at the knick-knack shop around across the road past the clothing stores, across the road again and round from her right through the crowd gathered around her in the tube station, back outside and back to the couple, she searched for a tall, dark-haired man bearing an umbrella and a newspaper.

But the odd couple were watching her again. And then, once they seemed to realise that they'd been spotted, they were very pointedly not looking at her again.

If she was being paranoid, she had a good reason for it, Susan realised slowly, staring at them unflinchingly now. Suddenly something in the almost embarrassed way the man's sunglasses-concealed gaze crept back towards her made her stiffen. Her stare sharpened, hardened. They were both the right height, yes, but surely—

The feel of someone's hand, briefly touching her shoulder, brought her swinging round. 'Excuse me,' a deep voice said, and she lifted her head slowly, taking in the expensive-looking, immaculately tailored dark suit, the conservative tie and pale shirt, the strong, cleft chin and firm mouth until she met a pair of the most vividly green eyes she'd ever seen. 'Should you be carrying an umbrella and a newspaper or do I have the wrong woman?'

Susan blinked. Tall and dark and wide-shouldered, he fitted his photograph broadly, but close up his size combined with the narrowed intensity of his green regard rendered him more...alarming than worthy of her sympathy. 'S-shouldn't *you* be?' she stuttered.

'What?' Two little lines appeared between his dark brows.

'Shouldn't you be?' she repeated, carefully this time. 'I

shouldn't. It's you who should. You should be carrying the brolley and the paper. That is if you're the one.'

'And am I? The one?'

His blank look reminded her that he was an orthopaedic surgeon. 'It's all right,' she said abruptly. 'The instructions were obviously too complicated. You are…Adam, I presume?'

'Adam Hargraves.' He took her gloved hand and shook it formally. 'And I should call you…?'

'Well, certainly not Sex Kitten,' Susan mumbled. 'Susan Wheelan. How do you do?' She twisted slightly and waved across the road at the couple in sunglasses. 'My sister Annabel. Her husband, Mike. I…I hope you won't take this personally but they appear to have come to spy on you.'

'Snap.' He drew her attention to another sunglasses-wearing couple who hovered on the corner by the men's clothing shop. 'My sister, Barbara. Her husband, Lawrence. Here, I presume, to ensure that they've not fixed me up with an axe murderer.'

Her eyes widened. 'They set you up for this?'

'Didn't know a thing until this afternoon,' he said heavily. 'You?'

'Same. Exactly the same.' She smiled, her breath coming out in a rush, the nervous tension which had gripped her since she'd agreed to this meeting lifting a little. 'Annabel wrote the reply to your advertisement and organised everything without telling me until today.'

'Barbara,' he told her. 'Advertisement, letters, the works.'

'And you're not…lonely and without friends or anything like that? You're not depressed? You're not…wasting away or pining for a wife?'

'None of the above.' He looked amused now and she

understood that—it was impossible to envisage a man who looked the way he did being any of those things.

'And you?' he asked calmly. 'Apart from being wet, you look self-contained enough, or underneath are you miserably lonely and unhappy and desperate to find a soul mate?'

'Not at all,' she said, hoping that her relief at escaping so easily from this meeting wasn't making her sound too gushing. 'I mean, I'm single and I'd like to meet someone one day but I'm so busy at work at the moment that I hardly have time to even think about it.'

'Then we're kindred souls.'

'Thank heavens for that.' She laughed. 'I feel silly now. I was worried you were going to turn out to be some pathetic lost creature whose ego would be devastated if I didn't show. Well, Mr Adam Hargraves, I'm glad you don't require my counselling skills.' Her relief had given her the confidence she'd badly needed. 'I'm sorry that you've had a wasted evening but for me it was actually a pleasure.' She shook his hand again, firmly this time. 'Goodbye.'

'Wait!' He'd let go her hand but as she turned back into the crowd he called out to her and she turned around automatically. 'Don't rush off like this,' he said, coming over to her again. 'Look, I'm going to have to take these two lunatics out for a drink.' He signalled vaguely towards the pair who were still watching them closely from the menswear shop. 'You're soaked. You need to dry out and get warm. How about the three of you joining us for half an hour? You'd be doing me a favour. Barbara's not the type to give up unless she sees we've made at least a token effort to get to know each other.'

'If she's anything like Annabel then you're right,' Susan admitted. His logic was superb although she was surprised that his orthopaedically geared brain had managed to come up with such a sensible idea. 'Well done.' Anything that would deflect Annabel from trying to match her with such an unsuitable man again sounded good to her, and with the two couples present she didn't have to worry about trying to make conversation with the surgeon. 'Yes, all right.'

'Give me a minute to collect my two,' he told her quickly, heading off that way. 'Meet you back here.'

She signalled to Annabel and Mike, but they kept turning around, pretending not to notice her, and in the end she had to physically cross the road. 'Idiots,' she hissed, becoming impatient as they still refused to acknowledge her.

'How did you know it was us?' Annabel protested, turning back with a startled look on her face.

'You look like something out of a horror movie,' Susan said sharply. 'Half the street is staring at you. Have you gone completely insane? What about the parents' evening?'

'We left early,' Mike explained sheepishly, removing his sunglasses to reveal pale, blinking eyes. 'Annabel got a last minute attack of the worries. She thought he might turn out to be a serial killer.'

'So...?' Pulling her sunglasses down a little, Annabel peered out at her over them. 'Is he?'

'He seems fine,' Susan told her. 'Not very bright, naturally, but that's all right. He's fine. But it's completely obvious to both of us that we're totally unsuited,' she added pointedly. 'Nevertheless, out of politeness he's invited us all for a drink.'

The introductions took a few minutes. Adam's brother-in-law, Lawrence, seemed friendly, but his wife, Adam's sister Barbara, appeared more wary of her. They went to an old-fashioned pub, which both Mike and Lawrence seemed to know well, a short walk away. There were a couple of seats left at a table and Annabel and Barbara took those while Susan and the three men stood a little away from them beside an artificial fire, sipping the drinks Adam had bought for them.

'So, Susan.' Lawrence stood very close to her, eyeing her rather as she thought he might a nice cake. 'You're a psychiatrist. That must be…interesting.'

She heard the hesitation and tried not to let it annoy her. On the walk to the pub he'd already revealed that he was an anaesthetist and she'd sensed more than a little of the condescension commonly accorded her own branch of the medical profession by the more hands-on areas. 'I think so,' she answered smoothly.

'Which hospital?'

'Four-tenths St Luke's and six-tenths St Martins.'

'St Martin's?' He waggled bushy eyebrows over her head at his brother-in-law. 'Now that is interesting.'

'We're both attached to St Martin's,' Adam told her quietly.

Susan nodded, not surprised that they'd not met before. Aside from the anaesthetists who covered ECT lists and the physicians to whom she referred her patients for advice on their medical problems, she didn't have a lot to do with hospital staff from the main hospital. St Martin's was one of the largest teaching hospitals in London and its psychiatric services, including the wards, outpatient areas and offices, were sited in a self-contained complex away from the main hospital itself. 'Did you train at St Martin's?'

'No, both at the London,' Adam said. 'And you?'

'University College,' she explained. It was warm close to the fire and her jacket was practically dry so she took it off, folding its tweedy bulk across one of her arms and hoping that the heat coming from the flames would dry the rest of her clothes as efficiently. 'I've only been at St Martin's for the last three years.'

He didn't say anything to that and she looked up quickly, stiffening as she saw his gaze slide slowly away from where her blouse still clung damply to the curve of her breasts.

Susan faltered, abruptly flustered. Unused to such brazen male attention, she wasn't sure how she was supposed to react. Mike had drawn Lawrence into an enthusiastic-sounding discussion of some approaching rugby international, leaving her alone with the surgeon. She flushed, then moved her jacket protectively back in front of her as she took several urgent sips of her cola, racking her brains to think of something else to say to him.

'Um…in your hobbies you mentioned scuba-diving,' she burst out finally, focusing somewhere a few inches in front of his face so that she wouldn't have to acknowledge the amusement with which his gaze had greeted her less-than-subtle gesture with her jacket. 'That must be…fascinating.'

But it seemed as if he wasn't as desperate to dissolve the thick silence that had grown between them as she'd been because he merely lifted one shoulder casually. 'Depends on where you dive.'

'And sailing,' she said firmly, readjusting the arm that held the jacket across her chest until she was sure she was safely and fully concealed. 'Where?'

'I haven't sailed in years.'

Behind them Annabel's raucous laughter pealed out and Susan glanced briefly over her shoulder, seeing, from their expressions, that whatever the two women were discussing they were clearly both enjoying themselves. 'But when you did,' she ventured, coming back to the orthopod. 'Sail, I mean. Once at least. Where?'

'Here and there. Would you like another drink?'

'No. No, thanks.'

His regard was utterly impersonal now and she felt herself relaxing a little. Telling herself that she was being ridiculous—that he couldn't possibly have been looking at her breasts because even an orthopaedic surgeon could not behave with such utter crassness—she rolled her jacket and deposited it onto the broad window ledge beside her.

Blinking down at her gently steaming blouse and skirt, she noticed that she'd managed to drain her cola already, but it seemed that Mike hadn't heard her refusal of the surgeon's offer of a new drink because he said cheerfully, to everyone, 'Same again?' Then he promptly headed for the bar, apparently not expecting any reply.

Annabel called out, 'Make mine a double.' Adam's sister echoed the comment, and Lawrence said something about helping him to carry things and headed after him. Susan registered rather unhappily that everyone except Adam and herself looked as if they were settling in for a long session.

Fortunately the obligation to make conversation with him lessened when Lawrence and Mike joined them again with more drinks. The three men ostensibly included her in their conversation about the rugby tour as the noise from the rest of the pub and the two women behind them grew increasingly more raucous.

Just as Lawrence announced that it was his turn to purchase another round of drinks, Susan heard Annabel use the word 'virgin'. Since the word was immediately followed by a squeal of what sounded like incredulous disbelief from Adam's sister, Susan turned around sharply. Both women immediately quietened and met her appalled stare so innocently that she decided she was being paranoid again. Annabel must have used the word in a context other than the one she'd assumed, she decided.

'I have to go soon,' she said abruptly, to no one in particular, although it was the orthopod who answered.

'I'll take you.'

'Of course you won't. I'll get the tube. It's not late and it seems to have stopped raining for the night.' Pleased that she'd sounded so briskly and efficiently confident, she checked her watch, then drained her drink with what she hoped looked like an equally determined gesture, only to be foiled by Lawrence pushing another full glass into her hand.

'I put a bit of kick into it for you this time,' he muttered into her ear. The noise in the pub wasn't so loud at that time that he couldn't have spoken normally but it seemed he felt the need to communicate privately. 'Something to liven things up. Taste it,' he urged. 'You'll love it.'

Susan doubted it. And she didn't need to taste it. One sniff was enough to make her eyes water. She tried to think of a polite way of declining the concoction but Lawrence had already gone back again to collect the other drinks. 'I rarely drink alcohol,' she explained lamely to Adam, realising that he'd seen the whole exchange and was now regarding her dispassionately. 'I don't like it.'

'I'll get rid of it for you.' With so little fuss that she suspected none of the others had even noticed the exchange, he took the drink away, returning seconds later with one that smelt reassuringly like pure soft drink. 'If you don't want it just leave it on the ledge.'

'Thank you.' She'd definitely imagined his earlier appraisal, she told herself, wondering if all orthopaedic surgeons would be as gallant as to come to her rescue the way this one just had. It was an old-fashioned trait that fitted well with orthopods' tendency to macho sexism, she recognised, but still she found it touching. 'I do want it,' she reassured him, not wanting to hurt his feelings when he'd gone to the trouble of buying it for her when it had really been her turn to buy a round.

He'd discarded his own jacket at some stage and rolled up the sleeves of his beautifully stitched shirt. Although the movement had only revealed the lower part of his forearms, she found herself noticing how strong and capable they looked.

The thought reminded her of the few times when, as a student, she'd been forced to attend Theatres to assist in orthopaedic operations. She winced. Apart from the grinding of the saws and drills, the hammering of mallets against chisels and the memory of the fine bone fragments the drills sent flying through the air in a misty spray, the thing that stood out in her mind was the ghastly popping, sucking sound that a leg made when the surgeon dislocated it from its joint.

Adam Hargraves lifted his drink to his mouth and she eyed the easy movement of his arm doubtfully. No doubt wrenching legs out of their sockets had contributed a fair share to the bulk of the muscles lying beneath his shirt, she reflected queasily.

'Your sister said in your advertisement that your other hobby was rugby,' she said, abrupt now, needing to distract herself. Lawrence and Mike had subsided back into their own sporting conversation again. 'Do you belong to a team or do you just enjoy watching?'

'I used to play. These days I'm too busy.' His eyes had narrowed on her face and suddenly the intensity of his regard hardened and it felt to her as if he'd made up his mind about something.

'How about taking these off?' He'd put his beer on the

ledge above the fire and now, to her befuddled astonish-
ment, his hands went to the arms of her large horn-rimmed
spectacles and lifted them gently off her face. 'You
weren't wearing them in your photograph.'

'What photograph?' She blinked dully up at the fuzzy
blur that was his face. 'Why did you do that?'

'Because I couldn't see you properly.'

She swallowed hard, abruptly nervous but determined
to keep her dignity. She could shout, make a scene, but
that would involve making a fool of herself, particularly
with Annabel and Mike only a few yards away. But without his co-operation the chance of her finding her spectacles was virtually non-existent. 'Could I have them back,
please?'

'Yes. Soon. When I've looked at you.' His cool hand
lifted her chin, tilting her face up to him. 'What colour is
that?'

'Just blue,' she said huskily, realising then that there'd
been no mistake about that earlier look she'd caught at her
breasts.

Unable to understand why the feeling of vulnerability
which he'd created in her so easily by removing her
glasses was now becoming not repellent or frustrating but
instead…oddly stimulating, she suddenly found herself
finding it hard to breathe normally. 'The shade changes a
bit in different lights. At least I'm told it does.'

'It does seem to,' he said deeply. 'Yes, they do change.
Right now they've turned very dark and very big.'

'Inside, too,' she told him. 'They're big, I mean.' She
took a deep breath, trying to calm her voice because it had
sounded wobbly. 'They're long at least. That's why I'm
so short sighted. You're just a pale blob to me at the moment.'

'So you should come closer.' To her mingled alarm and

nervousness his hands went to her shoulders and gently but insistently he drew her forward. He moved her jacket and sat against the window-sill beside him, meaning that she stood within the V of his thighs. 'Better?'

'Clearer,' Susan agreed faintly, because close to, like this, he was almost in focus again.

To her shock, his legs closed on hers, holding her still. When she realised that the sensation of being held imprisoned close to him wasn't at all unappealing, she froze.

'What's wrong?' he asked softly, obviously feeling the way she'd stiffened. When she didn't say anything he took her left hand, turned it palm up and stroked the inside of her wrist with his thumb. 'Susan? Am I making you nervous?'

'A little,' she conceded. 'No, actually, a lot. Could I have my glasses back now, please?'

His answer was to replace them carefully on her face. 'Better?'

'Marginally.' She sent a quick look sideways to where the other four sat, laughing and joking like friends who'd known each other for years. Clearly they were enjoying their conversation too much to have even noticed what was happening next to them.

She looked slowly back towards Adam. He still held her between his legs but was making no other move towards her. Having full vision back made her feel marginally less vulnerable but no less puzzled by the arousing effect he was having on her senses. She knew that she could break free of him any time—what she didn't understand was why she wasn't doing that. 'You're very sure of yourself, Mr Adam Hargraves.'

'And you have a beautiful mouth, Dr Susan Wheelan.' He spoke so quietly that she had to strain to hear him because the noise from the rest of the pub had now become a roar. 'Why don't you let me take you somewhere where I can touch you properly?'

Susan felt her head go muzzy. When she'd reflected earlier that day about good-looking men tending to be more insistent in their advances she'd not meant anything like this. She'd had difficulties now and then, extricating herself from overly passionate embraces, but no one had ever talked to her like this before. No man had looked at her mouth in quite this way until it swelled up as it felt as if it was swelling now. She didn't know what to do.

'I don't want to go anywhere with you,' she said faintly, wondering why at that moment it didn't seem as ridiculous an idea as it should have. 'We have nothing in common.'

'What we have in common isn't important,' he said softly, drawing her even closer, his arms low on her hips so that it felt as if she was encircled by him. He touched her forehead with his mouth, nuzzled her, she supposed it was called, only she couldn't be sure since no one had ever done that to her before.

'It's the differences that are important,' he continued, his voice very deep and very soft now. 'I'm a man.' To her utter bemusement his hands went to the top button of her blouse and he actually undid it, and she didn't offer a peep of protest. 'And you're a woman,' he finished, very, very softly, going for the next button. 'A beautiful woman.'

'You're trying to seduce me,' she whispered, blinking as much at his description of her as beautiful as at what he was doing to her, utterly dazed. 'You're quite, quite shameless. It's a Tuesday night. We're in a public place. We met less than two hours ago. Your sister and my sister are five yards away. And you're actually trying to seduce me. Are all orthopaedic surgeons like this?'

'Do all psychiatrists talk so much?' He was at her fourth

button now and as her blouse was high-necked he wasn't even down to cleavage yet, but she brought her hands up to stop him.

'This isn't a good idea.'

'You're wrong. It's a very good idea.' He didn't undo any more buttons but he gently eased aside the fabric he'd unfastened. 'A very, very good idea. I want to touch you,' he murmured, lowering his head again, shockingly tipping it so that he could press his mouth to the deep V of her throat. 'I want to take your breasts into my mouth.'

Susan gasped, unable to say a thing. She should have been shocked, outraged, horrified…disgusted, and in some ways she was all of those things but she still didn't pull away. In her entire life she'd never felt anything like the rush of heat his words and the determined, seeking pressure of his mouth sent spiralling through her.

Barbara, launching herself across them in a drunken blur, shattered the inertia which had held Susan frozen. 'Adam, you rat! Stop it. Leave the poor girl alone.' The older woman slapped at her brother's hands and arms. 'Let her go.'

When he did, finally, release her, his sister tugged her away. 'Poor Susan,' she tutted, patting Susan's head soothingly before she started fastening the buttons the surgeon had undone. 'Poor, poor Susan. Are you all right?'

'Fine,' Susan said faintly, wincing at Annabel's lopsided grin as the two women gathered around her in a sort of protective guard while the men seemed determined to head off Adam who was looking exasperated.

'Leave him alone for five minutes and he starts taking your clothes off.' Barbara sent her brother a disgusted look as she fumbled the final button on Susan's blouse. 'You poor little thing. Now you see where he gets his reputation from. You must have got such a shock. I'm so sorry we forgot about you.'

'I'm fine, really,' Susan protested, her head spinning, bewildered by both her own behaviour and the fuss the others were making. She craned her head but the two men were hustling the orthopod away to the bar.

She understood from the damp heat of her body that in those brief moments alone with him the surgeon had aroused her, but what she didn't understand was how it had happened.

While she'd never feared that she was the sort of woman to be permanently sexually unresponsive—her anatomy and senses were intact, there were no physical or emotional traumas in her past and she'd had a happy upbringing within a caring family—the fact that she'd never found a man's touch exciting before meant that she'd assumed she needed to be in love with a man for such feelings to develop.

It was something she'd been a little...proud of. If and when she fell in love it would make that relationship and the consummation of it very special. The fact that she'd responded now to a man who was not only a virtual stranger but also someone with whom she'd never forge any sort of intellectual or emotional bond challenged everything she'd thought she understood about herself.

'Should have left him to it,' Annabel was saying brightly, and Susan dimly noticed that her sister was swallowing the last of something that smelled like a very strong spirit. 'Considering that's supposed to be the whole idea of the exercise.'

'Susan's not that sort of girl,' Barbara told her, and Susan saw that the other woman's expression was reproachful. But clearly she couldn't sustain the mood because both woman immediately giggled. 'Honestly,

Annabel, you must have seen him,' Barbara said unevenly.
'Another five minutes and he'd have had her topless. A
man like Adam can't be trusted within ten miles of an
innocent like Susan.'

Susan felt sick. She looked at Annabel who promptly
went pink. 'I don't believe it,' she said dully. 'You told
her.'

'Susie, I had to.' Annabel looked upset. 'I had to explain,' she said defensively. 'Barbara thought you were
some sort of ferocious man-eater. She thought *Adam* might
not be safe.'

At that they both giggled again. 'It was the photograph,'
Annabel added. 'They misunderstood.'

'What photograph?' It felt like the umpteenth time she'd
asked it.

'One from Spain last year,' Annabel said airily. 'Just
you at the beach that first day.'

'Not...not in that hideous bikini?' Susan felt even more
ill. On the first day of their holiday she'd forgotten to pack
her swimsuit for the beach and as it was a ninety-minute
traffic-filled drive down from the villa they'd hired in the
mountains to the coast and far too hot a day to sit about
in clothes, she'd had to make do with Annabel's minuscule
bikini while her sister happily sunbathed in knickers.

Annabel, similar in size to her around the middle and
hips, unfortunately was almost flat up top and so the bikini
had been an embarrassment, merely covering the essen-
tials. Annabel had found Susan's embarrassment about
wearing the garment hilarious, and Susan wasn't surprised
to discover that her sister had managed to sneak a surreptitious photograph of the event.

'Tell me you didn't take a picture of me in that.'

'See what I mean about her being a prude?' Annabel
looked at Barbara who promptly nodded knowingly.

'You weren't wearing a bikini,' Barbara told her reassuringly. 'At least not all of it.'

Susan blinked. 'What does that mean?'

'It means that you looked great,' Annabel said, patting her shoulder drunkenly. 'Stop worrying. You rolled over when you were sleeping and I took a quick shot. It was just going to be a joke but when I saw how great you looked I realised how handy the picture might be one day. You've got a great figure, Susie. If you weren't such a prude you'd do much better for yourself. And the picture got Adam's attention, didn't it? That's what you wanted.'

'No. No, it wasn't.' Regardless of Annabel's level of intoxication, Susan couldn't let that one go. 'You know it wasn't. I never knew anything about him until today.'

'And now you do.' Annabel's beam suggested she'd announced something profound. 'Isn't that great? So? Wasn't I right?'

'I have an early meeting tomorrow. I really have to go.' Trying to talk sense with Annabel in her current state would be fruitless and frustrating, Susan decided, tensing as she saw that the three men, drinks in hand, were making their way through the crowd and back towards them. 'I really, really have to go. Barbara, a pleasure. Lawrence, nice to meet you. Adam…' She met the man's disturbingly enigmatic regard nervously. 'Well. Goodbye.'

'But you haven't finished your drink,' Lawrence protested. 'And we bought you a new one.'

Wordlessly she sniffed the glass he was holding to make sure it wasn't laced, then she lifted it and drained the liquid in a few quick swallows. 'Thank you.'

The orthopod promptly deposited his own untouched drink on the table. 'I'll drive you home.'

'I'm taking the tube.' Susan managed a teeth-gritting smile, but to her disgust the other four promptly drained their drinks in an apparent mimicking act and all five of them came after her to the pub's door.

'You've been drinking,' she muttered at the surgeon.

'Two pints of low-alcohol,' Adam told her calmly 'but we'll take a cab if that's what you prefer.'

'Not without all of us,' his sister declared. 'Poor Susan's not safe alone with you.'

'I'm not poor and I'm perfectly safe on my own so please, please, just go away, all of you,' Susan said tightly. '*All* of you,' she stressed, when Adam kept on coming forward.

'But we're trying to protect you,' Barbara told her brightly.

'Keep him with you and I won't need any protection,' she countered grimly, holding her hand out to fend them off. 'Mike,' she appealed, 'do something.'

Her brother-in-law looked surprised. 'Um…' he ventured. 'Well, Susan's right, you chaps. She's old enough to look after herself and if she says leave her alone, then that's what we should do. Now, my shout, is it? Doubles all around?'

To Susan's relief that seemed to be the miracle phrase because three of them reacted to that remark with obvious approval.

But the orthopod looked unmoved. 'Cab or car?' he said calmly.

'Tube,' she said finally, resigning herself. He looked too big for her to push away physically, at least until she had to, and too determined for her to waste time trying to dissuade him again. 'Definitely the tube. You're very persistent.'

'When I want something.'

Barbara clearly heard that because she turned back, her

pink face a picture of befuddled alarm, but Annabel caught her arm.

'Shush. Leave him alone,' Annabel muttered, audibly enough for Susan to start feeling ill again. 'They're fine. He's exactly what she needs. Do her the world of good.'

CHAPTER THREE

ADAM'S mouth quirked at the psychiatrist's softly muttered expletive as they left the pub.

'I swear one day I am going to kill that woman,' Susan said. 'Life imprisonment might just be worth it.'

They were away from the lights of the pub now but he could see that the set of her heart-shaped face was pale and tight. 'She means well.'

'She interferes.'

'She thinks she's helping.' He understood that much from years of trying to contain Barbara's best efforts to do the same sorts of things for him. 'She thinks she knows what will make you happy.'

'Well, yet again she's wrong.' He felt her looking at him, but when he turned his head she looked away hastily. 'And I'm sorry if I misled you back there. It was unintentional. You are a very handsome man and I do acknowledge that I allowed you to undo four of my buttons, but however that might have appeared at the time I didn't intend to encourage you. I don't make a habit of agreeing to sexual shenanigans with men I hardly know.'

Adam smiled. He understood now that he'd come on to her too strongly in the pub. He'd disregarded the fact that Annabel had set her up for their encounter in the same way that Barbara had set him up, and he'd allowed himself to be misled by the boldness of her letter and photograph.

He was irritated with himself for reacting the way he had but the way she'd looked when they'd met—hair damp and disordered around her shoulders, face streaming with water, her clothes wet and clinging to her incredible body—had driven every sane and sensible thought out of his head.

He'd felt himself captivated. He'd barely registered her manner, the way she spoke to him and the things she'd said. If he'd been able to do that, if he'd listened and been able to use his brain—instead of thinking with a far more insistent part of his anatomy—he'd not have needed Lawrence's fiercely whispered announcement at the bar when she'd been dragged out of his arms to know she wasn't as experienced as he'd assumed.

'The best thing for both of us would be if we simply forget tonight ever happened,' she added firmly.

'I can't do that.' Under the pretence of guiding her around the darkened corner they'd reached, Adam slid his arm around her back. Only he didn't release her once they'd changed direction. 'And I understand that you're not sexually...sophisticated. Lawrence explained.'

'Lawrence?' She stopped, her expression appalled. Her hand came up to push at his arm and reluctantly he was forced to let her go. 'Lawrence told you that? You mean Annabel told everyone?'

'If everyone means the three of us then I suppose she did.' In her obvious horror her mouth had opened, and he felt his pulse stir again as he contemplated kissing it. 'But, more accurately, Annabel told Barbara, and Barbara told Lawrence,' he amended. 'Babs is hardly the soul of discretion at the best of times. She'd never be able to keep her mouth shut about anything so...delightful.'

'Delightful?' Her echo had a sexy, husky edge to it. 'That's a different reaction. When Annabel found out she called me a freak.'

'She's your sister. Sisters say those things.'

'So you don't think it's so...abnormal?'

'Puzzling, perhaps.' Given her desirability and her responsiveness, as well as his knowledge of the single-mindedness of his own sex, her lack of experience did mystify him. But it didn't go anywhere towards taking the edge off his desire.

'I'm thirty-four years old.'

'You're saying…?' Adam touched the sensual fullness of her lower lip with his thumb, pleased that despite the startled widening of her eyes she didn't actually pull away from him. 'What?'

'That I'm too old for this.'

'Too old?' Moving deliberately slowly, he curled one hand around the back of her neck. 'For sex?'

'Too old for adolescent sexual experiments,' she said huskily, but he saw the widening of her pupils and felt the soft intake of her breath as he drew her fractionally closer.

'Is that what this is?'

'Isn't it?'

'I'm not an adolescent.' Although since seeing her photograph that afternoon he'd been reminded of how it felt to be one. He lowered his head, inhaling the faint floral fragrance that rose from the hollow of her throat. 'And I'm not experimenting.'

He brought his mouth down. 'You're so soft,' he murmured, almost touching her trembling mouth now, torturing himself by delaying taking what he wanted. 'Delicious.' He touched the bud of her lips with his tongue. 'Open your mouth.'

He knew that her inexperience might mean she needed gentle coaxing to rouse her to the level of responsiveness guaranteed to bring them both the pleasure he craved. He was prepared to cajole her, tease her into arousal, if that was required.

But what he wasn't prepared for, when his hand slid

down to cup one gloriously full breast, was her sudden shocked stillness then, seconds later, the unerring force behind the knee that swung up and connected accurately and painfully with his groin.

With a sudden out-rush of breath, he collapsed against the bricks of the building beside them. Before he could do anything, say anything coherent to stop her, she was at the kerb then in a cab and gone.

Lawrence looked heavy-eyed and pale the next morning when he wandered into Theatre's staffroom and Adam, irritated that his brother-in-law's tardiness meant his list was about to start fifteen minutes later than usual, regarded him unsympathetically. 'Heavy night?'

'The bar staff threw us out after closing,' the anaesthetist said miserably. 'Then Annabel dragged us off to some awful club. I've only had two hours' sleep. What happened with you two?'

'We're starting with case three,' Adam said evenly, ignoring him. 'The child who was supposed to be first has a cold so I sent him home. Case two was given breakfast so I've rescheduled her for last. Your SHO's looking after number three in your anaesthetic room.'

'And the lovely Susan?'

'Just get moving.' Registering the other man's unconcealed curiosity impatiently, Adam took a mask from a box on the wall and tied it hard around his face. 'My patient?' he reminded him pointedly. 'I'm the surgeon, you're the anaesthetist. I can't start until he's asleep.'

'OK, OK. I get the message.' Lawrence went off down the corridor, grumbling. 'But Babs won't let you off so easily,' he warned. 'She's worried. She doesn't want you near the girl. She's coming in to talk to you.'

Vowing to make himself unavailable, Adam pulled on

the protective goggles he wore while operating and went to scrub.

His registrar had already started. Washed and half-gowned, he was at the trolley, pulling on gloves, and Adam fastened the non-sterile ties at the back of the younger man's gown. 'What was the word from X-Ray?'

'The porters were just taking her down to Radiology for a scan of her calf when I left the ward,' Chris told him, referring to one of Adam's patients, a seventy-four-year-old woman with a fractured neck of femur, or top of her thigh bone, for which she'd already had surgery. She'd developed a slightly swollen right leg overnight. 'The radiology registrar's going to bleep me when he's finished. Do you really think it's a DVT?'

Adam sluiced his hands with water prior to soaping them. 'The probability's high enough to mean we have to rule it out,' he conceded. Their patient had reassured him that her leg was prone to swelling but he'd ordered the investigation regardless, not prepared to take a risk on missing a blood clot, or deep venous thrombosis.

He routinely treated his post-op patients with low-dose heparin and compression stockings and encouraged them to mobilise early to minimise the risk of such complications, but nothing could eliminate the risk of blood clots entirely.

'In all my time with you I've never seen a DVT on the ward,' Peter said.

'Unfortunately there'll one day be a first.' Having finished scrubbing, Adam swiftly dried his hands. A fractured neck of femur was an injury associated with a high mortality, even after, as in this case, it had been successfully diagnosed and treated. Around twelve per cent of patients died within three months of the injury—often from the condition which had precipitated the fall causing the fracture, such as strokes and heart attacks, rather than from the injury itself—and he tended to investigate and treat all of his patients very cautiously.

He hauled on a gown, staying still while he gloved so that the nurse who'd rushed to tie his gown could complete the task. After thanking her, he strode across to the table and gave the sterile tie knotted at the front of his gown to his scrub nurse who held it with a pair of forceps until he'd tied it around himself, completely enclosing himself within the sterile gown.

Lawrence had worked fast and his patient was anaesthetised. He'd been positioned lying on his front so that Adam could take healthy bone fragments from the man's left hip bone. Once he had enough, they'd turn him back onto his front so Adam could transplant the healthy bone into his right tibia where an old fracture had failed to join.

'We'll take it from the iliac crest,' he told Christopher. Valerie, his scrub nurse, had already partially swabbed the front of his patient and he and Chris now took over, using iodine solution to cover the man from waist to ankles. 'Guards.'

'Guards.' Valerie passed him the first of a bundle and Christopher took the other end. They opened it together and enclosed their patient's healthy leg, then the one they'd be operating on soon and then the man's back, followed by the area in which they'd work to extract the bone.

'Scalpel,' Adam ordered. 'Diathermy. Suction on?'

'Diathermy, yes. Suction connecting now.' Valerie passed him a scalpel. She was quiet while he made a small incision just below the prominence of the man's hip. But when she passed him forceps for separating the muscle fibres she added, 'So how was the blind date with the psychiatrist?'

Adam looked up from exposing the bone to send Lawrence an accusing look, but the anaesthetist immediately looked defensive. 'I didn't say anything,' he protested. 'How could I have? You know I only just got here.'

'Margaret told us but she decided you looked a bit dark this morning so she wasn't game to ask about it,' Valerie explained, mentioning the trauma unit's charge nurse, her brown eyes twinkling at him from above her mask. 'I'm older and braver. Come on, Adam. Spill the beans. We're all dying to know. How was it?'

'Curette.' Adam curled his fingers around the instrument and pulled it out of the nurse's grip. 'Saline gauze for Christopher. I'm taking the bone now.' As he collected the bone chips he scraped them carefully onto the damp gauze his registrar held. 'Another swab.'

Valerie, as he should have predicted, was persistent. 'Adam, don't be mean,' she said easily. 'Are you seeing her again?'

'Another swab,' he said tersely, a few minutes later. He pressed the swab to the edge of the bone he'd used. 'He's still oozing. I'm going to need some wax.'

'She was gorgeous,' Lawrence announced happily, as if they were still considering the subject of the psychiatrist. 'She must have been caught in the downpour just before we met up with her because her clothes were all wet and clinging and she looked...' He trailed off. 'Well, she's a real doll. A real number ten.'

Adam gritted his teeth. 'Table up,' he ordered. 'Move that light.'

But the task of adjusting the table height and focusing the light properly onto the wound only kept his brother-in-law temporarily distracted. 'You know she works here at St Martin's,' he told Valerie. 'Susan Wheelan. Know her?'

Adam saw from Valerie's shrug that she didn't but his registrar looked interested. 'Dr Wheelan?' he said. 'The psychiatrist?'

Adam, busy suturing the muscle back to cover the bone he'd revealed, ignored him, but Lawrence must have said something or nodded because Christopher continued slowly, 'I know her. At least I've heard her speak. She took us for a teaching session earlier in the year. Assessing the suicidal patient, or something like that. She was good. Nice legs.'

'Great legs.' Lawrence sounded pleased with himself. 'Mind you, if you think the legs are good you should see—'

'That's enough!' Adam glared at him. 'Cut it out, Larry. You're in my operating theatre, not your rugby club.'

'Defensive. Hmm.' Lawrence wiggled his eyebrows again. 'Not like you, Adam. Interesting.'

'Very interesting.' Valerie's eyes were still dancing a few minutes later when he was closing. 'So you fancied her, then?'

'Prolene for the skin,' Adam said tightly. 'Now.'

'All here waiting for you,' Valerie said lightly, passing him the thread on a straight needle. 'And did she?'

He quickly dressed the wound then, with the help of the other theatre staff, turned their patient over onto his front again and adjusted their positions and the siting of the diathermy and suction. 'Sandbag under his right buttock,' he ordered, stepping back and accepting the two new pairs of gloves Valerie offered him. 'Tourniquet on now. I want another two guards over the top here. Did she what?'

'Fancy you?'

He took a scalpel. 'Valerie—'

'All right, all right. I'm sorry.' She passed Christopher

more swabs but the way her eyes sparkled at Adam belied her apology. 'You can't blame us for being curious.'

'On the contrary,' he said heavily, nodding his thanks at Lawrence's signal that the tourniquet around his patient's thigh was now inflated, 'I blame you entirely.'

'You're our favourite bachelor,' Valerie told him. 'All the theatre nurses have taken bets on you. If you don't get married by the end of next year, I lose twenty quid. If you do, I win fifty!'

'Save time,' he said tightly. 'Pay up now.' He'd made a vertical incision over the site of his patient's tibial fracture and now, with his registrar's help, he retracted the muscle and tissues around the bone and slid a bone lever beneath it to expose the fracture itself. Carefully he cleaned around the rough edges of the damaged bone. 'Got those swabs?'

'Right here.' Valerie passed him the damp gauze. 'If the psychiatrist doesn't work out, how about I introduce you to some of my daughter's friends? Since her wedding, they all seem to have caught the bug.'

'How about you just concentrate on your work?' he muttered, gently packing the defect with the bone from the swabs.

'Barbara will get him married off,' Lawrence told Valerie confidently. 'You won't lose your money. He's her new project. She's got thirty-seven women on her list and they're all dying to meet him.'

Adam rolled his eyes. After the fiasco his sister had turned the previous night into, the chance of him allowing her to introduce him to any woman ever again was non-existent.

Once his graft was complete, he stabilised the area with a titanium plate, inserted a small suction drain and then closed. 'Above knee,' he told Christopher, referring to the type of plaster he wanted for the leg. 'Well padded and split it down to skin. The drain will come out tomorrow and we'll renew the plaster in ten days once his sutures come out.'

Making way for the metal buckets full of water which his registrar would use for dunking the plaster material, he drew back from the table. 'Good job,' he said. A quick glance at the wall told him they'd made up for the time they'd lost with Lawrence's tardiness. 'Chris won't take long to finish. May as well send for the next case.'

His list took them right through until one when they broke for lunch. While the others lingered in the theatre tearoom he went up to his office. But the sight of his sister perched on the edge of his secretary's desk and chatting animatedly immediately made him wish he hadn't.

'Thought you'd still be in bed and hung over,' he observed. 'At least I hoped you would be. To what do I owe the dubious honour of your visit?'

'Grumpy today, are we?' Levering herself off the desk, she beamed at him. 'I hear she had the good sense to throw you out.'

Impatiently he guided her into his office and away from his secretary's riveted expression. 'Out where?'

'Well, she didn't let you stay, at least,' she amended, looking smug. 'Annabel went around to Susan's flat first thing this morning to check on her and she was still in her nightie and definitely alone.'

'Is this conversation going somewhere or are you simply prying?' Attempting to resist the provocative image of the psychiatrist in something lacy and transparent, he bent to retrieve the files he'd come to collect from the cabinet beside his desk. 'If you're prying, you can go away.'

'I've found someone else for you. She sounds just perfect.'

'No.'

'She's a Capricorn. That's much better for you.' She looked pensive. 'I should have realised that Virgo wasn't right. I should have listened to my own reservations but I let Lawrence talk me round on that one. It won't happen again.'

Adam sighed. 'Barbara?'

'Hmm?'

'Get lost.'

'Adam, darling, I'm doing this for you,' she said with a firmness that he considered far exceeded any authority the four-minute age advantage she had on him gave her. 'You don't look after yourself properly. You work too hard. Everyone agrees that you need a wife.'

'I need a secretary and a housekeeper and occasionally a cook,' he pointed out reasonably. 'I have all three.'

He wasn't averse to the idea of marriage, but only if he met a woman to whom he could unreservedly make a life-long commitment. And he didn't share his sister's sense of urgency. Their own father had been in his forties when he and Barbara had been born and Adam's relationship with him, until his death, had always been superb.

'Just meet this girl.' Barbara passed him a photograph of a smiling, athletic-looking, *fully clothed* blonde. 'I promise you she's absolutely perfect for you. Isn't she pretty? Her name's Monica and she's a sports teacher. She loves diving and sailing and climbing and she's looking for someone who enjoys plenty of physical activity.'

'Forget it.' Adam barely glanced at the photo. 'No, don't forget it—try Christopher McInnes, my registrar. He keeps moaning about his awful social life. She's far nearer his age than mine.'

'Adam, stop this. Be reasonable.'

'I *am* being reasonable,' he said with what he thought

was creditable patience. 'Babs, for the last time, no more. I'll find my own women in my own time. I don't need your help.'

'You can't have Susan,' she said fiercely.

He blinked. 'Who said anything about Susan?'

'You don't have to say anything.' Her eyes had narrowed on his. 'I know you. But you can't, Adam, not Susan. Have a conscience for once. She's not like most women. She's…inexperienced. Just one look at her and I could tell she couldn't cope with you. Leave her alone. It wouldn't be fair.'

'Out, Babs.' Adam decided he'd had enough sisterly advice for the day and even, now that he considered it, enough for the rest of his life. 'That's enough,' he said tightly. 'Leave. I have to work.'

He half closed the door on her affronted expression. 'Chris's on bleep seven three one eight if you want to talk to him about your sports teacher. If you call him now you'll catch him at lunch.'

Susan didn't know what to do with the roses. She only had one vase. One of the huge bunches, two even, she could have coped with. But six? 'You'd better take these ones too,' she told her bemused-looking secretary when the hospital's florist delivered another bundle shortly before one. 'They'll keep all right in the sink with the others until you leave.'

Fresh and dewy, the old-fashioned red blooms which had been arriving all morning ranged in age from buds to fully open, but their scent was too exquisite to even consider her original determination to throw them in a bin. 'Is there a note?'

'Looks like the same as last time,' Rachel told her, smiling as she opened the small envelope which had been stapled to the Cellophane enclosing the flowers. '"Forgive me." And his bleep number again. How romantic. I can't believe you haven't called him yet.'

'I haven't called him because I'm never going to call him.'

'But what if you've left him emotionally scarred or something?' Rachel protested. 'Shouldn't you just call and explain why you don't want to see him again?'

'Being rejected by a nondescript psychiatrist is not the sort of event to scar a man like Adam Hargraves,' Susan said confidently. 'If you met him you'd understand. I can't imagine him ever going short of female attention.'

'So he's gorgeous as well as generous and thoughtful and obviously sensitive,' Rachel added, eyeing the flowers. 'I think he sounds divine.'

'He's fine,' Susan conceded. He was also single-minded and rather too forceful for her peace of mind but she wasn't going to think too much about that. 'He's just not…*me*,' she continued. 'So there's no point in either of us wasting time thinking about it.'

She checked her timetable and turned brisk. 'I'll be on Winchester Ward at the round if you need me. If any more flowers come don't tell me. I don't want to know about them. Just…get rid of them.'

The weekly full ward round at St Martin's main acute psychiatric ward was very different to normal hospital rounds. Instead of physically visiting each of their patients, the consultants, junior doctors, ward nurses and the other health professionals involved in the unit—the occupational therapists, physios, dieticians, social workers and community psych nurses—gathered in the large visitors' room at the end of the ward with the notes and they worked through the progress of each patient verbally.

They finished with one of Susan's patients, a fifty-five-year-old woman who'd been on the acute ward for three months with a long-standing and severe drug-resistant depressive illness but who she now considered was ready to return to the community.

'In summary,' she concluded, at the end of the more detailed run-through of Mrs Bibby's history which her registrar had presented, 'treatment of this admission has been successful beyond our initial expectations. Elizabeth's no longer suicidal. She's expressed optimism about the future and for the first time in five years has developed some interest in returning to work. She's done well on day visits out this week. I believe further time on the ward would be unhelpful. Roy?'

'Agreed.' The psych unit's charge nurse nodded his shaggy head. 'She needs out of here, man. And the time can't come too soon.'

Susan could see that the remainder of the hospital staff agreed, but the community social worker, a relatively new addition to the ward's circle of associated personnel, looked unhappy. 'Dr Wheelan, twelve weeks ago Mrs Bibby tried to hang herself in her building's communal laundry,' she said hesitantly.

'I'm sorry, but she was also behind on the rent for months before I found out about it and her landlord is determined to formally evict her from the premises. I've tried to explain to him that she was ill for a little while but now she's well again, but someone told him that she's had shock treatment and he seems to think that means she must be insane. I've tried but either he doesn't understand or he doesn't want to understand. He's got tenants lined up for her flat and he's threatening to sell her possessions to pay the rent she owes. Our halfway houses are full until the beginning of next month and there's no emergency housing available. If you discharge her she doesn't have anywhere to go.'

Susan sighed. Her job—returning her patients to good mental health—these days seemed invariably complicated by the social issues that compounded their problems. It was only rarely that she could discharge any of her longer-stay patients into a stable, safe environment, and that meant that she had no beds on the wards for acute emergencies. 'If you give me the landlord's name and number I'll try and speak to him personally,' she said evenly. 'Might that help?'

'Worth a try,' the younger woman said doubtfully. 'The word "doctor" can sometimes work miracles that we can't.'

'Does she have any family?' Duncan Dilly, the consultant in overall charge of the unit, looked concerned.

'A brother in Cardiff who's not interested,' Susan said quietly. 'Also an ex-husband, address unknown, who cares even less.'

'Do your best.' Duncan's grimace suggested he understood as well as she did that there were few alternatives. They had one long-stay ward plus two supposedly acute wards with forty-eight beds between them, but of those almost thirty were taken up by people no longer needing emergency treatment who were simply waiting to go elsewhere.

As the meeting dispersed, Duncan came up to her. 'Tomorrow night,' he reminded her. 'Seven-thirty.'

'Fine, yes.' Surprising herself after the depressing tone of much of the meeting, Susan even managed to summon a smile. 'I'm looking forward to it.' Duncan was giving a talk at the medical school on the history of psychiatry and she'd agreed to lend her support. It wasn't a hardship. What he lacked in dynamism as a speaker he made up for with superb research and presentation and she always enjoyed listening to him.

'Duncan, do you mind if I ask you something personal?'

'I invariably dislike that question.' They were walking back down the corridor that connected the wards with the block containing Outpatients and their offices. He sent her a dry little smile. 'It's so loaded, you see. If I say yes then I offend you. If I say no then I'm exposing myself to heaven knows what.'

Susan smiled, acknowledging there was some truth in that as she went through ahead of him into the foyer of the other building and towards the stairs. 'It's nothing heavy,' she said reassuringly. 'I just wondered if in all the time we've known each other you've ever thought about kissing me.'

They were almost at her office now but he stopped short of the door. 'That's "nothing heavy"? Susan—'

'I don't mean that I want you to,' she said quickly, seeing that she'd embarrassed him. 'I'm not propositioning you. I simply wondered if you'd ever, even once, considered it.'

'Frankly, no,' he said quietly. 'You're a beautiful young woman, Susan. You'd never be interested in a dusty old thing like me.'

'You're neither dusty nor old,' she countered, blinking a little bemusedly at the realisation that it was the second day in a row that someone had referred to her as beautiful. 'And how do you know I've never been interested?'

'It's obvious,' he said sounding far more confident than she felt. 'I have been married, remember. I do know a little about how women work. You've never wanted our relationship to be any different from the way it is.'

'But how do you know that?' she insisted. 'How can

you know for sure? I might think I don't want it to change, but when it actually happened I might feel differently.'

'What on earth are you talking about?'

She bit her lower lip, wanting to explain but not finding the words easily.

Unlike Annabel, she'd never had an exciting social life. At school and later at medical school her studies had seemed more important than the opposite sex, and as a junior doctor she'd had little opportunity to think of anything but work. She'd dated occasionally over those years—enough, she'd thought, to build up the small shell of experience which had led to what she thought was her understanding of herself and her responsiveness but she'd never dated any man more than once.

Since her appointment as a consultant at St Martin's and St Luke's three years ago, she'd theoretically had more time for dating, but working in the narrow specialist field of psychiatry she rarely met any eligible men. Apart from a few unsuccessful dates set up by well-intentioned friends or Annabel, most of her outings had been with Duncan.

The fact that she hadn't fallen in love with him puzzled her. He was a lot older than her, true, and he had two adult children and had never expressed any interest in having more, but in every other way they seemed ideally suited. So why, when their friendship was strong and she deeply admired the incisiveness of his intellect and his professional achievements, had she still failed to develop any feelings more emotional than bland fondness combined with a gentle appreciation of his quiet company?

Her response to Adam Hargraves the night before played on her mind. Was she, in fact, a far more sensual person than she'd ever imagined? Or, more alarmingly, did…abstinence eventually make one's body less discriminating about when and to whom it chose to respond?

More pertinently, since it seemed the part of her capable of responding sexually to a man had definitely changed, was the failure of her feelings for Duncan to progress simply a product of neither of them having yet made any move towards extending their relationship?

'My brain may think I don't want you to kiss me,' she told Duncan finally. 'but if it happened I might discover that my body actually liked it. The experience might be different to the anticipation of the experience.'

'Who have you been reading?'

'No one. Nothing.' She could hardly explain the reasons her curiosity had been aroused. 'I'm not talking about any type of psychological theorem. I've just been thinking.'

'Curious thoughts.' To her frustration, when she'd hoped that he might have been able to help answer some of the questions the night before had raised, he merely studied her with brief puzzlement, before gesturing for her to precede him into the office area.

'What beautiful roses,' he remarked, and Susan saw that he was eyeing the stacks of blooms on Rachel's desk with the appreciation of a connoisseur. 'Rachel, is it your birthday?'

'That was two weeks ago, Dr Dilly,' the secretary told him evasively, exchanging a befuddled look with Susan when the other psychiatrist bent to sniff the blooms. 'Nine,' she mouthed over Duncan's shoulder, her eyes wide and incredulous. 'Nine!'

'Then happy birthday for two weeks ago,' Duncan told her, straightening again. 'I'm only sorry I didn't realise earlier. Their scent is delightful, isn't it? My mother used to grow some very similar when I was a boy. It's hard these days to find roses that smell like this.'

'Take some for your office.' Seizing a bunch, Susan ripped away the note that had been stapled to them and thrust the flowers at him. 'Please,' she insisted, when he hesitated. 'We've far too many here. And some for Anita,' she added, taking away another note and giving him another bundle for his secretary.

'And one for Winchester,' Rachel added, removing another note and passing him the last bunch still on her desk. 'They might brighten the awful place up for a few days.'

'This is most generous.' But Duncan's attention was on the notes that Susan had scrunched up into her palm. 'Thank you, both. So they're not for your birthday, Rachel?'

'No, they're for me,' Susan said carefully, honesty and an unwillingness for Rachel to be placed in an awkward situation forcing her to admit that, although she'd rather have kept the information private. 'Only I don't want them.'

'I see.' He looked interested. 'An admirer, Susan?'

'Not at all.' She didn't believe that Adam Hargraves could be called that, at least not in the sort of old-fashioned way Duncan would have meant. 'Duncan, I've a session at five with the Wilson family. We're videoing it for the students. I was hoping to use seminar room one. Is that all right with you?'

'Of course. I'll take room two.' Room one, the one he normally used for his registrar-teaching sessions scheduled for the same time as Susan's student sessions, was the best equipped for taking videos. While both rooms had two-way mirrors concealing observation rooms, in one the mirror was less intrusive and she'd noticed that her patients generally seemed less self-conscious.

'But leave a note on the door,' he advised. 'The St Luke's registrars have developed an irritating habit of arriving late recently.' Gathering his roses, the psychiatrist sniffed them again appreciatively. 'Goodbye, ladies.'

Rachel waited until he was out of sight. 'Nine,' she said incredulously. 'Nine bunches. Susan, you have to call him. You know you do. Whatever he did, just forgive him. If you don't, the flowers might never stop coming.'

'I'll bleep him after my next session,' Susan said wearily, admitting, finally, that she couldn't allow the situation to continue unchecked. 'I don't want to interrupt his working day now. We'll exchange apologies and then he'll stop these ridiculous deliveries and this will all be over. All right?'

'You'll *exchange* apologies?' Rachel looked intrigued. 'Why? What did *you* do?'

'I...' She realised she could hardly explain about being panicked into using her rusty self-defence skills to escape him without explaining why, and that wasn't the sort of conversation she wanted to provoke. 'We...both... There were faults on both sides,' she said.

'Interesting.' But when Rachel saw that Susan wasn't going to elaborate, she shrugged. 'But I'm glad you're going to speak to him. Think of how much these must all be costing. The poor man might go bankrupt.'

'Surgeons are never poor,' Susan reassured her, depositing the crinkled little envelopes containing the orthopod's notes in the bin by Rachel's desk. 'He probably earns your pay and mine in his first hour of the week in his private practice.'

Rachel beamed. 'So he's a good catch, then?'

'If money's your only criterion then, yes, I imagine he is.' Susan rolled her eyes at her secretary's avid expression. 'It's not one of mine and you're happily married,' she reminded her sternly. 'Which may not make any difference to Mr Hargraves but your husband might object.'

Rachel brightened anew. 'So he's that irresistible, then?'

'No.' Surveying her secretary's intrigued expression from the doorway of her office, Susan sighed. 'Of course he's not. I'm resisting, aren't I?'

CHAPTER FOUR

ADAM and Christopher went directly from Theatres to the wards. 'We'll go round Churchill and Chamberlain, then kids and George and finish on Trauma,' Adam told his registrar as they hurried up the stairs. 'Any news from Casualty?'

'Two admissions—one eighty-year-old woman with a fractured neck of femur, following a fall at her home, and an eleven-year-old with a displaced fractured distal radius and ulna who Warren is doing under GA in half an hour,' Christopher explained, mentioning one of Adam's SHOs. 'We'll keep him in tonight and let him home in the morning.'

'What about the first case?'

'Theatre's booked for seven.' They were at the fourth floor now and Christopher led the way left onto Churchill Ward. 'I thought I'd do an Austin-Moore,' he said, referring to a type of half-joint replacement where the surgeon simply replaced the top of the badly damaged thigh bone with a prosthesis. It was a straightforward, quick procedure with a low complication rate. 'She walks locally to do the shopping and so on but otherwise she's not very active,' he said, explaining why he'd chosen not to replace the whole joint. The films should be up here by now from Casualty. I'll show you.'

Confirming his registrar's comments, the X-rays showed a fracture through the narrowing at the top of their patient's thigh bone. 'You're right to go for an Austin-Moore,' Adam commented, tracing the uneven line of her fracture with one finger. 'Surprisingly the hip here's not too bad. How is she otherwise?'

'Relatively fit,' Christopher reassured him. 'She had her appendix out when she was thirty and a hysterectomy for fibroids twenty years ago but no other admissions. No medical problems and her heart and lungs are fine.'

At the bedside, Adam questioned Mrs Sylvan on the fall that had broken her leg.

'No, I didn't get dizzy or anything,' the frail-looking little woman said waveringly. 'Jenny just ran right in front of me and I tripped. She had her tail twisted around my leg and I couldn't stop myself. If I've told her once I've told her a hundred times, don't run around me when I'm going down the steps, but she never listens.' She looked up at him quizzically. 'Still, she's a good friend. I couldn't wish for a more pleasant companion.'

'Cat,' Christopher said in an undertone.

Adam, who'd already guessed that, sent the younger man a dry look as he crouched to check Mrs Sylvan's pulse. 'She sounds good company.'

'Yes. Yes, she is.' She tilted her head and regarded him rather as he thought her cat might have done. 'She's ninety-one,' she told him. 'Cat years. Exactly to the month. Older than me. She's done very well. No broken legs at least.'

'You're going to be here for at least a month with yours,' he said quietly, moving to examine it. Presently in a splint from Casualty, it was still two inches shorter than its partner and twisted slightly outwards. 'Perhaps even longer. You'll need intensive physiotherapy to help you get used to walking on it again. Is there someone who can look after Jenny for that long?'

'The neighbours are good,' she told him. Lifting her

head a little off the pillows, she regarded her leg doubtfully. 'Will it be the death of me?'

'I don't think so.'

'Wouldn't it be better chopped off?'

'No. Mr McInnes is going to fix it for you,' Adam explained, nodding to indicate his registrar. 'At seven. It's a
straightforward, commonly performed operation. He's going to replace the top of your leg with a metal model.
Tomorrow you'll be able to sit in a chair. By next week
I'd like to see you walking.'

'I'll do my best, Doctor.'

'Good.' He checked gently under her eyes, pleased that
she wasn't too pale.

'Haemoglobin's twelve,' Christopher told him. 'Electro-
lytes and clotting normal.'

'Very good. Well done.' Adam smiled. 'Your iron levels
must be good. You're not a vegetarian, then?'

'Jenny and I both like a nice piece of steak,' she said
happily.

After the wards they went to the trauma unit and Adam
regarded their emergency admission from the day before
thoughtfully. Conscious and lucid, his fractures stabilised
and now off the ventilator, he was ready for transfer to an
ordinary ward.

'Tony, according to the notes my house officer took
from her telephone call to your relatives after you were
admitted, you've suffered from depression in the past.'

'I've been on medication,' the young man acknowledged dully after a long pause. 'Not for two years. The
doctor said it was because of me being made redundant,
and after I got a job again the doctor told me I was cured.'

'What doctor?'

'GP,' he said finally.

'Have you ever seen a psychiatrist?'

Again Adam thought that he might not answer but eventually he said, 'Nope.'

'And this accident yesterday…?'

'Don't remember.' His patient lifted one shoulder in a vague shrug, but the way he still refused to meet Adam's eyes worried him. 'The bike slipped,' he muttered, after another long hesitation. 'I don't remember.'

'The police said that your bike's a write-off,' Adam said quietly, watching him.

Rather than showing any of the concern he'd hoped to see, the young man merely shrugged again, still avoiding his eyes.

'How were you feeling before the accident?'

The silence stretched once more, but finally his patient mumbled, 'Family rows. No different to usual.'

'I'd like you to see a psychiatrist,' Adam told him. 'I'd like one to assess you to make sure that you're not depressed. If you are then that may have contributed to your accident.'

'If I have to.'

Tony looked particularly indifferent to the idea, although beside him Adam sensed his registrar's sharp look.

'Duty psychiatrist?' Christopher asked, at the end of the round.

'Susan Wheelan,' Adam ordered. He wrote her bleep number on a sheet of notepaper which he'd found at the nurses' station then passed it to the younger man. 'History of depression. The road was dry at the time and conditions were good. There was no alcohol in his blood and his urine screen was clear. Ask her to see him as soon as possible. Now, if possible, before he's transferred to the ward. The nurses can watch him closely here but they're too busy on Churchill.'

'Dr Wheelan may not be the day's duty psychiatrist.'

The registrar, Adam noted, looked curious. 'Shouldn't we refer to the on-call doctor?'

'She lectured you on it so it must be her field. I don't want the duty psychiatrist—I want her.' Irritated by the feeling that he had to explain himself to the other doctor, Adam pulled rank. 'Susan Wheelan and only Susan Wheelan.'

'Understood.' The sideways shrewd look Christopher sent him suggested that he still harboured questions about Adam's motives, but the way the younger man went promptly for the telephone told him that at least he wasn't brave enough to confront him with them. 'Do I mention your name or is the source of this referral supposed to be a secret?'

Adam made an impatient sound. 'Do whatever you have to do to get her to see our patient,' he said tersely, turning on his heel. 'Ask someone to bleep me when she arrives.'

The referral from a registrar on the trauma ward came as a surprise to Susan. Her session with the Wilson family had just finished and she'd used the telephone in the observation room. She frowned, watching the technician who'd operated the camera disassembling the lights in the seminar room as she wondered what best to do. 'I'm not on call today,' she explained hesitantly. 'Shouldn't you be talking to the duty psychiatric registrar?'

'I should be, but my boss particularly asked for you, Dr Wheelan.'

'Your boss?' Susan frowned. 'Who is...?'

'Adam Hargraves.'

'Oh.' Susan wondered why she hadn't guessed that. Orthopaedic surgeons and trauma. The connection made sense. She took a deep breath. 'In *your* opinion, Mr

McInnes, and I don't mean in your consultant's opinion, in *your* opinion is this... Tony Dundas suicidal?'

'In my opinion there are genuine grounds for suspicion,' he replied. 'He's been depressed. He appears depressed now. The road was dry, he's an experienced motorcyclist, he hadn't been drinking, his tox screen was negative and the driver of the lorry told police that he seemed to swerve straight into his path.'

The registrar had answered promptly and fluently but Susan still frowned, not quite ready to allow herself to be completely reassured. 'Does he really need to be seen immediately?'

'On Trauma we have one and a half patients per nurse,' the voice came back. 'If he goes to Churchill, there are at least eight per nurse, often more. We can arrange for him to be specialled by the nurses if you think it's necessary, but in order to justify the expense of one-on-one care we need to have a psychiatric opinion about the appropriateness of it before he's transferred.'

'All right. I'll come,' Susan agreed slowly. 'I'm here at St Martin's at the moment and I can come across to the main hospital directly. Explain to me where the trauma ward is.'

'Third floor, surgical block,' he said. 'Turn left inside the main entrance and the lifts are just along the corridor. Thanks, Dr Wheelan. See you soon.'

After thanking the technician for his help in recording her session, Susan collected the video he'd recorded and quickly returned to her office to deposit her notes and the tape.

'Twelve,' Rachel told her cheerfully, gesturing to some more obviously recent deliveries of roses. 'I've promised a bunch to all the secretaries. They're going to collect them as they leave. Have you called him yet?'

'I'm going to speak to him now.' Susan's teeth clenched. If she found that the referral he'd made was fudged, they'd not only be exchanging apologies, she'd be giving him a stern talking to as well. She was too busy to tolerate her time being wasted. 'I'm going over to the main block,' she said tightly. 'I've been referred an inpatient on one of the surgical wards. Rachel, don't bother waiting around for me to get back—you may as well finish now. Any calls?'

'Two reps, one reminder from your registrar at St Luke's that your team's supposed to be presenting a case at their grand round next Monday and she wants to know who to prepare, and Mrs Bibby's landlord—who you wanted me to find for you—won't come in to see you but he did say he'll be home Friday evening if you've got something to say to him.

'Also, Derek Coleman's been admitted to St Luke's. He's acutely psychotic apparently. The on-call registrar says do you want to see him tonight? Only they've had to sedate him and he's sleeping now so you might not get much sense out of him.'

Susan sighed. Derek Coleman was a young patient of hers who had schizophrenia. On his last admission a year earlier she'd changed his medication and she'd thought he'd been doing very well, but obviously things had deteriorated since his last appointment. 'I wish someone had called to let me know he was unwell earlier,' she said wearily. 'OK, I'll leave seeing him until tomorrow.'

She spent all day Tuesdays and Wednesdays plus Thursday and Friday afternoons at St Martin's, but the rest of her week was based at St Luke's, a small sister hospital to St Martin's about a thirty-minute drive away. 'Fit the reps in when you can. I know about the grand round and she can prepare Mrs Henderson's case to present, and fine with Mrs Bibby's landlord. Let me know his address and I'll call in on him on Friday night after my clinic.'

She ducked into her office, deposited the video and collected a notebook and pen.

'I thought I'd leave a note for the florist in case there are more deliveries after I go,' Rachel told her when Susan emerged from her office again. 'Just in case you can't stop him sending them. Where shall I say to leave the roses?'

'Have them sent to the wards.' At least that way the nurses would put them in water and people would get enjoyment out of them. 'Hopefully there won't be any more. If he's got any sense he'll have decided that twelve bunches is message enough.'

'You've had more roses today than I've had in my lifetime,' Rachel said wistfully. 'Perhaps he's fallen in love.'

For the first time since the whole dismal episode had begun, Susan laughed. 'You,' she said easily, checking her watch as she went for the door, 'are a true romantic. Sorry to disappoint you but there's no potential for romance here. To put you out of your misery, last night he…' She hesitated over how best to put it, but Rachel came to her rescue.

'He propositioned you?'

'He's obviously not used to being turned down, but he was so now he sees me as a challenge to his manhood,' Susan finished, nodding her relief that the other woman understood. 'It's silly, I know, but true. Men like him are very easy to read. These flowers are part of his ammunition.'

'But they're not working?'

'Not remotely.' Susan was very certain of that. 'I'm simply not interested. See you tomorrow.'

Unused to spending any time in the main hospital, the layout remained a mystery to her despite the years she'd worked on the site but, following the instructions of Adam Hargraves's registrar she found the trauma unit easily enough.

She peered through the plastic doors from the small changing suite outside, where she stopped to wash her hands and don a protective cotton gown, relieved to see that the only staff in the eight-bedded unit appeared to be nurses. There was no sign of Adam Hargraves.

Her clothes covered, she went inside and towards the main desk. 'I'm Susan Wheelan,' she told the smiling woman who'd looked up at her approach. 'I'm one of the psychiatrists here. Christopher McInnes called me to ask me to see Tony Dundas.'

'Tony, yes, bed one. Hello, Dr Wheelan. I'm Margaret Barton, charge nurse here.' The other woman passed her a set of notes but kept looking at her, smiling—inspecting Susan with what Susan felt to be a puzzling amount of curiosity. 'I know Adam's very worried about him.'

'Really?' Susan pursed her lips, still unsure about how far she was willing to trust the surgeon's reasons for the referral. 'Then I'm surprised he didn't discuss the case with one of my colleagues yesterday.'

'Tony only woke this morning,' the charge nurse explained. 'He was ventilated post-op and overnight.'

'And his injuries…?'

'Fractured pelvis, right humerus and both legs,' she recited cheerfully. 'He's stable now. Adam's keen to transfer him upstairs to Churchill.'

'And your impression of his mood?'

'Depressed,' the nurse said firmly, nodding as if to reinforce her words. 'He's not interested in anything. He won't eat and he hardly communicates.'

'Family?'

'A father and brother and sister in London but none of

them have been in to see him. No girlfriend or wife. He hasn't had any visitors.'

'Thank you.' Susan had been briefly scanning the notes while Margaret was speaking, and now she snapped them shut and tucked them under her arm. 'Bed one, you said.'

'Off to the right. You have privacy for your talk because he's our only conscious patient at the moment.'

The older woman bustled around the desk. 'You know, I hope you don't mind me saying this, but you're far younger and…softer than I'd expected.' At Susan's startled look she added hastily, 'To be a psychiatrist, I meant. Are you very new to the job?'

'I think I'm probably older than you're assuming,' Susan said unevenly.

'But, then, Lawrence did say you were very pretty.'

'Lawrence?' Susan blinked, realising that she hadn't been feeling unreasonably paranoid about the thoroughness of the nurse's inspection. 'Anaesthetist Lawrence?'

'He's one of the directors of our little unit,' the nurse explained with a smile. 'He said that you all had an…interesting evening last night.'

Susan pushed her glasses up with a tremulous finger. 'I think I'd better just see my patient,' she murmured faintly.

'We're all very fond of Adam here,' the nurse continued. 'Very fond. But, having raised two daughters of my own, I suppose I'm naturally protective when I hear….' The nurse trailed off, then came back with, 'Well…Dr Wheelan, you will be careful, won't you?'

'I really think I ought to see my patient,' Susan said hastily, her face prickly with heat, mortified that she'd obviously been the subject of discussion between Lawrence and the nurse. 'Please.' Her hands were shaking. 'Now.'

'Of course. This way.' The nurse sent her a little beam as she pulled the screens around the bed, giving them a little more privacy. 'Open your eyes, Tony,' she ordered. 'We know you're not asleep. This is Dr Wheelan, the psychiatrist we told you about.'

Susan spent fifty minutes with him. Not an unusual length of time for a full psychiatric assessment, although she usually tended to work faster than that, but Tony Dundas was complicated.

When she finally emerged from behind the screens she was preoccupied, and the sight of Adam Hargraves standing behind the desk, regarding her broodingly as she approached, barely made an impact on her.

'You were right,' she said slowly, 'to call me.' Aware of their patient's proximity, she looked around, seeking an office or side room. 'Is there somewhere we can we talk?'

'Of course.'

He directed her to the side corridor off the main unit but, slowly becoming aware of him again, Susan sent a mildly alarmed look back towards the nurses gathered by one of the other beds. 'Perhaps the charge nurse—'

'Margaret's busy,' he said calmly, one hand curling around her arm disturbingly to guide her away. 'She's about to go off duty. I'll pass everything on.'

'Well, first of all, he's definitely clinically depressed,' she said unevenly, finding herself in what looked like a medical office behind the main unit a few moments later. Her legs were feeling a little weak and she took the chair behind the desk gladly, giving him a few seconds to settle onto another seat across from her. 'You were right about that. And he's certainly suicidal. While what happened yesterday doesn't appear to have been premeditated, it was certainly not accidental.'

'He deliberately crashed his bike?'

'It was a spontaneous suicide attempt following an argument with his father, yes,' she confirmed, studying the pharmaceutical slogan written along the side of the pen she'd been using rather than meeting his disturbingly intense regard. 'But his problems stem from events far further back than that.' Briefly she ran through the psychiatric history she'd extracted from his patient.

'So, in summary, you're looking at a long history of low self-esteem and suicidal ideation beginning in early adolescence following the death of his mother. He won't discuss what happened to her but I sense that the event was very traumatic. It seems to have triggered some sort of breakdown in his relationship with the rest of his family, from which many of his problems have evolved.

'This argument with his father occurred on his only meeting with the family in over six months. He's had two prolonged episodes of depression, the first of which was managed by his GP using a tricyclic antidepressant, but he's had no treatment with this current episode which seems to have lasted about six months. He's preoccupied with thoughts of suicide and my primary concern is that he's not so physically depressed that he lacks the motivation to carry them out, as we see from what happened yesterday.

'Now, what about all those pins and loops and pulleys and traction things?' She managed a quick glance up. 'And that metal triangle thing sticking out of his hips? He needs to be on a psychiatric ward with specialised psychiatric nursing. Can we get rid of the metal?'

His eyes narrowed. 'Those pins and metal and that triangle *thing* are holding his pelvis and his legs together,' he said heavily. 'And unless you can cope with his pelvis and legs falling apart then, no, you can't get rid of them. He needs to be on an orthopaedic ward. I'm not risking that equipment on unskilled nurses.'

'I'm quite willing to admit that I don't have a clue how

to cope with a falling-apart pelvis and legs,' she countered huskily, 'but the man is a danger to himself on an unsupervised ward.'

'He's pinned in,' he observed. 'He can't move off the bed.'

'If he's determined enough he can do anything,' she argued. 'He's quite capable of forcefully disconnecting himself from that...traction stuff. He needs supervision.'

'I can arrange special orthopaedic nursing or, if you feel that won't be sufficient, you could supply psychiatric nurses to special him,' Adam said briskly, obviously unwilling to compromise on moving Tony anywhere but to an orthopaedic ward. 'So, what does he need? Therapy? Antidepressants?'

'Antidepressants to counter his clinical depression, together with careful monitoring by trained staff,' Susan told him tightly. 'Therapy, yes, of a problem-solving nature at first. Later something deeper aimed at giving him insight into the effect of his past and at improving his self-esteem,' she explained. 'But nothing works immediately. His primary need now is a safe and secure environment. How long will he be in all those...traction bits?'

'Approximately twelve weeks.'

She hesitated. 'We should start seeing an improvement from his antidepressant medication quite quickly,' she explained. 'It used to be said that changes took at least three weeks to appear, but our thoughts are changing on that now. But we won't necessarily see a rapid change in his suicide risk,' she added. 'I'll ask the psych unit's charge nurse to give your nurses a refresher talk about management of the suicidal patient. I should be able to get budget authorisation for two nurses a day from us to be with him if you can supply the night staff and meal staff from Orthopaedics.'

'Sounds reasonable.' He leaned forward abruptly, and she pushed herself back in her chair. He sent her an amused look and she realised that he was merely going for the telephone beside her.

'See how much we can achieve when we co-operate?' he remarked evenly once he'd punched out the numbers and was apparently waiting for a reply.

Susan ignored that. 'When will he be moved off this unit?'

'He's probably been taken up already. I'll let Churchill know he needs to be specialled tonight until you have a chance to sort out the psychiatric staff.'

'I'll just write up the notes. He needs some blood tests, too. We do some screening routinely in depression. His basic results are here, I see, but I need to check his thyroid function and B12 and folate levels. I'll leave the forms with his notes.'

Her self-consciousness seemed to have soared and Susan saw that her hands were shaking again as she opened Tony's chart. She flicked through the notes clumsily, searching for the current page, aware that the surgeon was still watching her as he passed on his orders to someone on the other ward.

When he'd finished his conversation she forced herself to lift her head and confront his gaze. 'By the way, we don't call supervision by our psychiatric nurses *specialling*,' she said formally. 'We call it *continuous care*. Our nurses develop a therapeutic relationship with their patients. They don't merely supervise them.'

'I'll remember that,' he said gravely.

'You needn't wait,' she added quickly, trying to sound sure of herself, which wasn't easy given that her voice had taken on a distinctly nervous tremor.

Annoyed with herself for her cowardice, she acknowledged that she had to postpone mentioning the roses and apologising about her behaviour the night before. She wasn't confident she could do either with any sort of composure right at that moment. Both would have to wait until she was feeling more herself. 'This'll take ages,' she added huskily. 'I'll finish here and take the notes to Churchill myself. Where is it?'

'Up one floor,' he said evenly. 'But there's no rush.' To her dismay he pushed his chair back and stretched his legs out in front of him, obviously quite relaxed. The way he slid his hands into his pockets suggested he had every intention of waiting until she was finished. 'I don't have plans.'

Wordlessly she returned to her work, but a few minutes later she looked up again, meeting his speculative regard with an anxiety she knew she hadn't been able to conceal. 'Please, stop.'

'Stop what?'

'You know what I mean.' When he didn't react she crossed her feet uneasily. 'I understand that you're probably used to women falling about all around you but…I think you should have realised by now that that's not going to happen with me.'

'I came on too strong last night,' he said evenly. 'I'm sorry.'

'You did and you should be and your apology is accepted. And I'm very sorry about…what I did. I…overreacted, I'm afraid. I hope I didn't hurt you too much.'

'The discomfort was transient,' he told her, his regard unflinching. 'The discomfort from your knee, that is.'

Susan felt her flush darkening as the possible meaning behind that remark occurred to her. 'Please don't send any more flowers,' she said, wanting to move away from the subject of his pain very quickly. 'I've nowhere else to put them.'

'When you've finished here I'll take you to dinner.'

'No.' She dropped her eyes. 'No, you won't.'

'Tomorrow, then.'

'Not tomorrow either.'

'Friday.'

'No.'

'You don't eat?'

'Please, don't force me to be rude.' She rested her pen on the desk and stared at it fiercely. 'I assumed I'd made my opinion clear enough last night.'

'You were giving out mixed messages last night.' In contrast to her, he sounded utterly calm. 'You still are.'

'I'm not interested.'

'Then why are you becoming so emotional?'

'I'm not becoming emotional,' she retorted, pleased by the irritation that curled through her because it was enough to smother her self-consciousness. 'I'm simply…stunned speechless by your arrogance.'

Delighted that now, finally, she sounded firm and strong, she collected the notes together and stood. 'I'll finish this outside. I'll organise one of our nurses to come to Churchill tomorrow morning and I'll let the on-call staff know about him in case there're any problems overnight. I'll chart an antidepressant for him to start tonight. I'll follow him up regularly and if you need any information, *professional* information, I believe you've demonstrated that you know how to get in touch with me. Goodbye.'

'Stunned *speechless* is a terrible exaggeration, Susan Wheelan.' To her horror he moved fast enough to actually grab her free wrist as she made to go past him. 'You do far too much talking and thinking and not enough feeling. Why are you so frightened about eating with me?'

'It's not the food I find frightening—it's you,' she hissed, tugging ineffectually at her arm as she glared down at him. His grip was firm, but although he wasn't hurting her she couldn't seem to free herself. 'I get the definite impression that it's me who's supposed to be on the menu.'

'The idea has a certain…appeal,' he admitted lazily, his thumb sending disturbing little shivers across her skin from where it stroked her wrist. 'But I promise to feed you first.'

The deepness of his voice, the warm amusement in his eyes, the smooth, soft movement of his thumb, made her feel as if she were going into a trance. 'I bet you were very spoiled as a child.'

'Babs and I were spoiled horribly,' he agreed. 'Our parents married late. They'd thought they were too old for children so we were a wonderful surprise.'

His grip tightened marginally and she steeled herself to resist him pulling her down onto him on the chair, but instead, in one supple movement, he uncrossed his ankles and came up onto his feet, backing her against the wall behind her. 'I didn't want for a thing.'

'It's very obvious.' She stared up at him, miserably mesmerised by the emerald amusement of his gaze. 'Has anyone ever refused you anything?'

'I don't remember it happening.'

'That doesn't surprise me in the slightest,' she whispered. 'We are completely incompatible.' Her head was starting to spin again in the confusing way it had started to spin the night before. 'We have nothing in common. Nothing even to talk about unless you count our patient.'

'I haven't stopped thinking about your mouth.' His voice was so husky now that it rasped against the rapidly heating skin of her throat. 'And your breasts. Your legs—'

'Adam, I don't want to hurt you again,' she protested, wishing she felt outraged instead of…bemused, dismayed by how weak her voice was sounding again. 'But I promise I will if you don't stop this.'

'Spend time with me,' he murmured, brushing aside her hair to bring his mouth close to her ear. 'If you're so sure we're incompatible, prove it to me. Anywhere. Any time. Pick somewhere you'll feel safe.'

'And would I be?' She twisted her head, lifting her shoulder to force his mouth away, his breath too disturbing against her ear. He hadn't kissed her, and he held her lightly, barely touching her, but she seemed to be shivering uncontrollably. 'Would I be safe?'

He was still for a few seconds. 'Sure you want to be?'

She stiffened, realising, appallingly, that at that moment she wasn't completely certain of that. There was a terrible sort of excitement in his embrace, a sense of pulse-thudding disquiet in the knowledge that for once in her life she wasn't completely in control of a situation.

The sensation wasn't at all unpleasant.

It was an acknowledgement that shocked her and so she tried to deny it, striving for the sensible. 'Yes,' she said finally. 'Yes, I'm sure. I definitely want to be safe.'

'Then, naturally, you are and you will be.'

Slowly he withdrew from her but there was nothing safe about the way he was looking at her and it made her burn.

Tonight would be impossible. She could barely look at him. 'Tomorrow,' she said huskily. He was right that seeing him socially once at least would be a chance to put things in perspective, an opportunity to demonstrate to him how profoundly unsuited they were.

'Duncan, a…colleague, a friend of mine, another psychiatrist, is giving a lecture at the medical school,' she said unevenly. 'The Pasteur lecture theatre.' Seeing the two men together, particularly when Duncan would be at his sharply intellectual best, would be a welcome reminder of the surgeon's inadequacies in that direction, she realised. It would be a chance to get her...physical response to him in perspective. 'Seven o'clock,' she added thickly. 'Afterwards, if you're still interested, we could all have something to eat together.'

'All?' Like he'd done the night before in the pub, he brought his thumb up to rub at the swollen curve of her lower lip. 'You mean the three of us?'

'You said that I should feel safe,' she said, bringing up the notes she still gripped in her left hand to cover her breasts because they seemed to be growing tight and sensitive.

She held her mouth firmly closed but still he probed the corners with his thumb, his vivid eyes narrowed intently on the movements of it against her. 'You feel you need a chaperon?'

Four of them hadn't done her much good the night before, she acknowledged, but that didn't mean she was willing to risk being alone with him. 'Duncan and I always have dinner after these lectures,' she told him. 'We're close friends. We often...go out.'

'How close?'

'Very.'

Susan turned her head away from his descending mouth but her gasp was enough to give his thumb access to her mouth and when she tried to twist her head back he lowered his head sharply and kissed her, hard, his tongue sliding against her where his thumb had probed.

'Seven o'clock,' he confirmed, and she saw when he lifted his head that, whereas she felt flushed and hot and utterly shaken, his colour was completely even and he wasn't even breathing fast.

Moving away from her smoothly, he opened the door.

'Finish writing up in here, if you like. It's Lawrence's office. He won't mind you using it.'

Susan didn't move until she heard his footsteps heading back towards the main unit, and then she spun quickly, shutting the door behind him with deliberate care when what she most wanted to do was slam it violently.

She hated being at a disadvantage but with that kiss that was where he'd coolly put her. She normally hated not being in control yet she hadn't been in control since the moment she'd met him. But most of all, she fretted, she hated feeling vulnerable. Yet Adam Hargraves had just made her feel as if she were on the verge of walking naked and unarmed straight into an enemy's camp.

Was she being melodramatic? Paranoid? Or was her anxiety, as she very much feared, entirely sane and sensible?

CHAPTER FIVE

WALKING back onto the trauma unit after leaving Susan in Lawrence's office, Adam met Margaret's concerned look speculatively. 'Thought you were due off duty an hour ago.'

'I was worried about that poor girl,' she countered, peering down the corridor towards the offices. 'What have you done with her?'

'She's not poor. She's not a girl. And she's more than capable of looking after herself.' Coolly he eased the set of notes she clutched away and out of her hands. 'She's writing up her interview with Tony. What are these?'

'New patient just up from Cas. Not one for you. An ICU surgical case, only they're full. Since we've four beds free, Lawrence OK'd the admission. An ICU nurse is coming across.'

She took back the notes he passed her but he saw she was still studying worriedly the corridor he'd just emerged from. 'I hope you haven't been up to anything naughty, Adam. Lawrence will be unbearable if you've made his office untidy.'

'Lawrence is always unbearable,' he observed dryly. 'Stop fretting, Margie. She's not a child and you're not her mother. Go home.'

'Innocence is a very precious thing these days, Adam. I wish I could believe that you realised just how precious.'

Adam realised why he was having so much trouble convincing her not to worry about the psychiatrist's well-being. 'Lawrence,' he grated, irritated with himself for assuming the anaesthetist could keep his mouth shut about anything. 'What's he running here? A ward or a news network?'

'He doesn't mean any harm,' Margaret said hastily. 'And you know he's not very good at keeping secrets. What did Dr Wheelan think about Tony?' she added immediately in what he knew was a transparent attempt to distract him. 'We've already taken him upstairs, but what did she think?'

'Suicidal and depressed,' he said heavily, wondering how much Barbara would miss her husband if he were found mysteriously strangled with one of his own ghastly elastic-necked ties. 'As we suspected, his accident wasn't an accident,' he said, meaning Tony. 'Churchill nurses will have to special him until Susan can organise psychiatric nurses to take over two shifts a day.'

He recognised that he couldn't actually murder Lawrence but infuriatingly he realised that he couldn't even say anything to him because any comment would simply increase the anaesthetist's already over-stimulated curiosity.

'Home time for you.' Hands on Margaret's shoulders, he turned her around and propelled her out of the unit, determined not to allow her to interfere by interrupting Susan despite the concerned glances she kept sending past him and along the corridor. 'She's fine and you work too hard. Get out of here.'

Susan was at St Luke's on Thursday morning rather than at St Martin's. She spent the morning on the wards in meetings, firstly with the staff and later in individual sessions with the patients who'd been admitted under her care, and it was lunchtime before she made it to her office.

The sight of a large collection of Cellophane-wrapped

roses piled haphazardly outside her door brought her to a dismayed stop.

She'd had enough, she decided wearily. Enough of roses, enough of harassment from Annabel who was still determined to extract from her every detail about her encounter with the surgeon and enough of being distracted by brooding thoughts about Adam and her peculiar reaction to him.

Her mouth tightening as she contemplated how the orthopod could possibly have found out where she'd be that morning, she vowed to have a stern talk with Rachel.

She collected the flowers and stomped inside, pulling one of the labels free from its Cellophane as she marched to her desk. She opened the note, checked the surgeon's bleep number, called St Martin's and had him paged.

However instead of Adam, the voice which answered after a few seconds belonged to someone who introduced herself as Theatre receptionist Mary Lee. 'I'm afraid he's operating right now,' the young-sounding woman said brightly. 'I can take a message for him or if it's an emergency I can send someone into his theatre to interrupt him.'

'It's not urgent,' Susan said hastily, deciding that perhaps it was better not to speak to him directly anyway. The man had a way of distracting her in ways she didn't appreciate. 'Would you please tell him that the lecture he was planning to attend tonight is cancelled.'

'The lecture tonight,' the receptionist repeated laboriously, sounding as if she was writing down the words.

'Well, actually, not the lecture itself,' Susan amended. 'That's not cancelled, no, not at all. Just say that his *invitation* to the lecture is cancelled,' she added, deciding that her first words had been less honest than she was comfortable with. 'His invitation to the lecture and dinner—please, mention the dinner, that's important—is cancelled.'

'Dinner,' the bright voice echoed. 'Cancelled.'

'And I'm Susan Wheelan,' Susan told her. 'Or just write Susan. He'll know who I am.'

'Susan Wheelan.' There was a brief pause and then the receptionist added, 'Susan Wheelan? Is that Dr Wheelan, the psychiatrist?'

'It is,' Susan conceded guardedly, surprised that a theatre receptionist would be familiar with her name.

'Oh, Dr Wheelan, I'm so pleased to speak to you,' the other woman promptly gushed, increasing Susan's bemusement. 'I'd like to tell you how much I admire you. I think you're an amazing woman.'

Susan blinked. 'Really? Have you…been to one of my lectures or just read some of my papers?'

'Oh, no, nothing like that.' There was a giggle. 'Oh, I'm not that brainy. I'm not a nurse. I just answer the phones and do the filing. I mean that I admire you for the stand you've taken. I mean I really admire you for that.'

'The stand?' Susan was more bewildered. 'On what?'

'On yourself,' the receptionist chirped, leaving Susan no more enlightened. 'It can't have been easy. Especially since everyone says you're so pretty.'

'Well…thank you.' Nonplussed, Susan wasn't sure what else to say. 'That's very…um, I'm not sure I understand.'

'I mean it would be easier to understand if you were hideously ugly,' the voice continued cheerfully, 'but if you look as good as people say you do then you must have had loads of offers. I just think it's amazing that you've turned them all down. I mean, you must have been tempted but you just never gave in. I think that's great.'

Susan felt sick. She felt the way she'd felt when the trauma unit's charge nurse had started talking to her about

Adam. 'I still don't think I understand,' she said slowly, desperately hoping that she didn't.

'I really think that virginity's something very special these days,' the voice replied promptly. 'I only wish I'd realised sooner. I mean, I had sex with my first boyfriend when I was fifteen. Now that I'm twenty I look back and that seems scary. I was really taking risks with myself, doing that. I mean, even if you don't think about the health problems, I wasn't psychologically ready for that sort of thing.'

Susan's fingers crumpled the orthopod's note without any conscious thought from her. She opened her mouth, unsure of exactly what she was going to say, but the younger woman didn't let her get a word in.

'I should have waited,' she continued brightly. 'Really, until now I didn't realise that I was just letting men exploit me. I thought nothing of getting my clothes off for them, but when you do they just take you for granted. I can't tell you how much it meant to me to hear about you yesterday. I really thought a lot about things last night on my way home. Hearing about you has changed my life. Last night I told my new boyfriend that I wasn't going to sleep with him any more. I told him that he could just wait until I was ready again. I told him he had to sleep at his own place until I'm psychologically prepared for him.'

Susan's face felt as if it were on fire. 'Mary, are you sure this is what you want—?'

'Oh, don't worry, Dr Wheelan. I know what I'm doing. I just want to thank you for giving me the idea. I'm taking a stand. I'm going to respect my body from now on and my boyfriends are going to have to respect it, too. And if they don't like it then they can just move on.'

'Well, I hope that works for you,' Susan managed, aware that her voice sounded strangled. She said a quick goodbye then lowered her head into her hands, aware that she was shaking.

It couldn't be as bad as she was thinking, she told herself weakly. It couldn't possibly be that bad. This…Mary person had simply overheard Lawrence and Adam talking as they'd walked into Theatres.

The knowledge that the two men had been discussing her was unsettling, but she told herself that the orthopod's lack of discretion supplied proof—*if* she'd needed it—that there were no grounds whatsoever for any relationship between them.

She reminded herself again that the unhappy fact that one theatre receptionist and very probably one trauma unit charge nurse knew about the state of her hymen did not mean that any other member of hospital staff knew. There was no need to feel paranoid.

She called Annabel and left a terse message on her answering machine about disloyalty and careless talk and gossip and what she thought of sisters who blithely revealed private secrets to virtual strangers, but the acidic speech did little to make her feel better.

Despite her determination not to, she was still feeling paranoid that evening as she helped Duncan set up for his evening lecture. The weekly event was sponsored by various drug companies who supplied supper for the attendees. The company rostered for the evening had a reputation for the generosity of its food budget so the hall was full of students and resident junior doctors, along with a smattering of the usual senior staff, all helping themselves to plates of sandwiches and mini-quiches and sausage rolls.

Although rationality told her that their attention was on their food, Susan still felt self-conscious as she counted through Duncan's slides to check they were all there in preparation for his lecture. No one knew, she told herself fiercely. No one knew. No one knew who she was or anything about her. Or at least only a very few people could possibly know.

When she'd finished checking the slide numbers she collected Duncan's notes and put them up onto the lectern beside her, then took the slide carousel again and carried it up, her head lowered, to the top of the theatre to the technician in the projection room who'd be responsible for screening the pictures and adjusting the lecture hall's lighting.

She found a seat for herself in one of the sparsely occupied back rows, exchanged a smile with Duncan, who was waiting down the bottom ready to begin his lecture, and sat down.

As the lights dimmed and Duncan stepped up to the lectern, his bespectacled eyes lowered to the notes, Susan leaned forward tensely, finding herself anxious on his behalf, willing him to do well.

'Ladies and gentlemen, welcome to tonight's lecture,' Duncan began carefully. 'I'm going to talk to you about the history of psychiatry, a history you'll come to see is as bloody and brutal as the evolution of modern surgery from barbershop butcherism.'

Susan blinked, a little surprised by the uncharacteristic drama of her colleague's opening but pleased that the hushed stillness of his audience suggested he'd at least managed to capture the attention of the students.

'Indeed, in the later part of the fourteenth century, St Mary of Bethlehem Hospital here in London, later known as Bedlam, was merely a series of dungeons where the rudimentary psychiatrists of the day occasionally roused themselves enough to practise ritual tortures more mutilating than even the most enthusiastic and adventurous barber surgeon,' Duncan continued.

There was shuffling at the other end of Susan's row, followed by movement, and seconds later a man eased himself into the seat next to her. 'A promising start,' a voice said quietly close to her ear, 'for a lecture that was supposed to have been cancelled. Susan Wheelan, you are a shameless liar.'

'I didn't say it was cancelled. I said *you* were cancelled,' she hissed after a sharply indrawn breath, unpleasantly aware of the sudden stiffening of what felt like her entire body, including—especially including—her mouth which he was studying and which suddenly felt about a foot wider than it was and hard to move naturally. 'Why are you here?'

'Improving my mind?'

'Not before time,' she mumbled, half to herself in an undertone but not apparently as inaudibly as she'd assumed because the regard that lifted from her mouth to her eyes was definitely amused.

'It's just lucky for me that you're here to translate the long words.' Shockingly he shifted his hand to her skirt-covered knee, which he squeezed.

'I'll photocopy you a transcript,' she bit out, pushing his hand away sharply and returning her eyes very pointedly to Duncan, hoping the surgeon got her message. 'Circle the words you don't understand then look them up in a dictionary.'

'Indeed, after the relative enlightenment of earlier cultures, the Dark Ages in Europe signalled a regression in psychiatric practice,' Duncan announced happily. 'Treatment became the domain of priests skilled in exorcising demons and persecuting witches. Victims exhibiting signs of what we now know as schizophrenia were brutally tortured into confessing to witchcraft then punished by death.'

He clicked on a slide and Susan frowned at the graphic

horror of the picture. It showed an obviously terrified thin young woman being restrained by what looked like a frenzied mob while grinning monks stacked kindling about her feet.

'If the burning provoked a confession the victims were stoned to death as punishment for their sorcery. If it didn't then it was assumed that they were definitely witches and so they were either weighted with stones and thrown in a river or burned at the stake. Those who survived were immediately publicly executed.'

His next slide was greeted by a collective gasp from his audience, and Susan shuddered and averted her eyes, the painting of a bloodied, pale corpse being retrieved by an eager crowd from a river too horrific for her.

'The bodies were retrieved to check for death then thrown back into the river and left to the fishes,' Duncan explained cheerfully.

Susan realised that Duncan sounded as if he was enjoying himself. Normally a subdued and intellectual rather than an emotional speaker, he was tackling his subject with a gusto she'd never glimpsed before.

'Naturally, none of these treatments provided a cure for psychiatric illness within the community,' he continued, 'although, given how widespread the persecution of victims appears to have been, they certainly must have reduced the prevalence of mental disease.'

He beamed at them expectantly, perhaps waiting for a chuckle at that comment, but the audience remained silent and Susan suspected that, like herself, the majority of his listeners were too aghast to muster a reaction.

'He's having fun,' Adam remarked close to her ear when Duncan paused for a few seconds to show another unpleasant slide. 'Bit of a sadist, your friend, is he?'

'Don't be ridiculous,' Susan hissed. But she was frowning.

'A common delusion of the time was that victims considered themselves wolves. This was vigorously treated with an amputation of an arm or a leg to prove to the victim that he or she was human. Fortunately, the eighteenth century signalled a turn towards the more humane treatments of earlier ages and other civilisations, although a popular theory of schizophrenia still held that insanity was a result of evil deeds and therefore appropriate treatment was restraint and punishment.'

'Do you think the pictures are necessary?' Adam growled, when Duncan showed another horrific picture of someone being tortured.

'He's simply being thorough,' Susan said weakly. 'He's a professional. This is a highly intellectual discussion.'

'A later therapy involved rotating patients violently in a spinning chair,' Duncan announced. 'It was believed that the massive shock generated by being spun so rapidly would interrupt the victim's morbid preoccupations, which were assumed to be the cause of the victim's insanity.'

'He really is enjoying this,' Adam insisted when Duncan continued on in the same fashion. To her horror, he squeezed her knee again. 'I'd watch out for him if I were you.'

'You're being absurd,' she said faintly. She pushed away the hand that now lingered disturbingly on her thigh, crossing her legs away from him so there could be no accusations of double message-giving. 'Please, stay quiet. I'm listening.'

He was quiet for most of the rest of the lecture, although from time to time she felt the brush of his gaze against her face, a face she kept firmly averted, concentrating hard on Duncan's speech where normally it was no effort at all to listen to him.

There was enthusiastic applause at the end and her colleague took a few questions—rare, in her experience, after his talks—and then they joined him down at the front of the hall.

Duncan, she saw, looked rather flushed. 'A good response I thought,' he said brightly, sending her a pleased little smile as he collected his files together. 'The crowd was rather enthusiastic tonight.'

'Because you were...incredible,' Susan assured him, still more than a little bemused by his presentation. 'I didn't realise you were so enthusiastic about the history of psychiatry.' Conscious of Adam looming behind her, she swivelled to introduce him, finding herself a little awkward. 'Duncan Dilly, this is Adam Hargraves. Adam's an orthopaedic surgeon here at St Martin's. I...well, I suppose you could say that I invited him to your talk.'

'Mr Hargraves.'

'Adam, please.' Both men shook hands. Adam's expression, she decided, was unreadable, while the older man's gaze darted between him and Susan before he eyed the other man interestedly.

'An enlightening talk,' Adam commented. 'Your special interest?'

'It is something of a hobby.' The technician had come down with Duncan's slides and the psychiatrist thanked him for his help as he took them. 'In fact, I've been approached to write a book on the subject.'

'I didn't know that,' Susan exclaimed. 'Duncan, you didn't say anything.'

'It's nothing extraordinary,' he explained. 'Simply a small text for medical students.'

'But still.' She directed her gaze to Adam. 'Duncan is

a prolific author,' she told him. 'We're very proud of him in the department.'

'Just a few contributions to textbooks,' Duncan said quietly. 'One or two papers this year, that's all. You've done as much yourself, Susan.'

'Not the same calibre of publications,' Susan countered.

'You've years ahead of you,' Duncan dismissed. 'Now, Lawson's, shall we?' he said, naming the restaurant at which he and Susan regularly dined after the lectures. With a nod to the other man he added, 'Adam, are you joining us?'

By the time Susan had thought about that and opened her mouth, intending to say very firmly that he wasn't, the surgeon had beaten her by murmuring a quick affirmation and he merely smiled at her frustrated glare.

Both men stood back for her to precede them out of the hall and she went ahead reluctantly, wishing she could think of a way of extricating herself from the dinner without hurting Duncan.

To her surprise it seemed that the two men weren't as incompatible as she'd assumed they would be. By the time they'd completed the short walk across the medical school's compound to the restaurant they'd fallen into an amiable discussion about the English cricket team which, it seemed, was abroad on tour.

Because there were three of them they couldn't take their usual table by the window, and the beaming waiter directed them to the tiny restaurant's one remaining unoccupied booth. Susan slid into the bench seat closest to the wall and looked pointedly towards Duncan, intending him to sit beside her so that they'd both be facing Adam, but her colleague was busy inspecting the blackboard menu on the wall and, with a bland look, the surgeon moved in beside her.

'Cosy,' he observed, his thigh coming against hers as he sat, she was convinced, far nearer than even the limited size of the booth demanded.

'We like it,' she said tightly, squashing herself against the wall to break the contact between them.

'The steaks are very good,' Duncan told him, sliding in opposite them. 'We've been coming here weekly for two years and I haven't been disappointed yet.'

'Two years?' Susan saw Adam's brows rise as he contemplated that. 'What about you, Susan? Have you been...disappointed in that time?'

'Not that I recall.' Ignoring the other possible implications behind that question, Susan turned her attention pointedly to her menu. 'I usually have the salmon. It's always good.'

When a cool hand encircled her knee as the first course was being delivered she realised that the meal was going to go very badly for her. Adam had ordered soup, leaving his left hand free to roam unobtrusively across her leg, while she, unwilling to embarrass Duncan or herself by making a scene and needing both hands above the table to manage her pasta, could only send him an occasional glare of impotent rage.

'After so many pleasant evenings together, I think of this restaurant as *our* restaurant,' she said pointedly to Duncan during a break in the cricket discussion. Until then she knew that her own contributions to the conversation had sounded stilted and awkward but this time she strove to keep her voice bright. 'Our *special* restaurant,' she emphasised. 'Don't you, Duncan?'

'No, not really.' She'd hoped for some sign, however token, of possessiveness from the psychiatrist but Duncan disappointed her. He blinked, appearing a little surprised by her question. 'It's just the most convenient one to the hospital, isn't it?'

As if punishing her for using such transparent tactics, the hand on her knee slid higher to her thigh where it lingered. 'Surely you mean the most convenient one with the best food?' Adam said mildly.

With a proprietary air that infuriated Susan he proceeded to signal for another bottle of the mineral water she'd just drained.

She did her best to avoid looking at him but he forced her to by leaning against her and dabbing at the edge of her tight mouth with his napkin. 'Tomato sauce,' he murmured, surveying her stormy expression mildly. 'Gone now.'

Susan knew now that she'd been wrong to assume that Duncan's presence would curb some of the surgeon's outrageous behaviour. In the time it had taken her to swallow a few half-hearted mouthfuls of her spaghetti, he'd firmly and insistently inched her skirt high enough up her thighs to mean that the only barrier between his caresses and her skin was the thin nylon of her tights, and at the same time she knew that he'd just made his intentions clear to the one man she'd thought might be able to rescue her.

More frustratingly, instead of Duncan raising any objections to this, he was merely observing the pair of them with a sort of benevolent regard more suited to a kindly uncle than a threatened suitor. 'You'd go a long way to find better food,' he agreed.

Her salmon was superb but although the arrival of his steak had forced Adam to take his hand away from her leg she was still overwhelmingly conscious of him—of his thigh against hers, the brush of his arm against hers as he moved, of the possessiveness in his gaze that brushed her face—and she could eat little.

The hand came back after he'd finished his meal and he sent her what she interpreted as a gently chiding look, before deliberately easing away the fabric of the skirt she'd gathered up and firmly sat on and lifting it again.

Taking advantage of Duncan being distracted at last as he complimented the waiter who'd returned to clear the table, she sent the surgeon a furious look, but the sole outcome was that he merely shifted the hand he'd installed firmly across her lower thigh fractionally higher.

'I suppose you're finding this very amusing,' she murmured grimly, not looking at him again and not even trying any more to push his arm away and her skirt down because she knew that the hand would come back immediately and that there was nothing she could do if she didn't want Duncan noticing what was going on.

'It's not amusing me in the least,' he replied deeply. His thumb stroked softly across the inside of her thigh, turning her unbearably tense. 'When we leave I'll tell you exactly how you're affecting me.'

'Dessert,' she said abruptly, prompting raised eyebrows, she saw, from both Duncan and the waiter who weren't used to her ever demanding such a thing. 'Um…may I see the menu, please?'

'Of course, Doctor.' The waiter looked pleased. With a flourish he produced a small folder listing the choices. 'And may I recommend the chocolate *gelato*, made freshly this evening?'

'You may, thank you—that sounds delicious.' Susan snapped the folder shut. 'I'll have that. And coffee to follow.'

Both Duncan and Adam ordered coffee as well which they both drank fairly efficiently but, by lingering over her dessert and then sipping only very slowly at her own coffee, Susan struggled to draw the meal out. Guiltily aware that Duncan, unused to their evenings going on this late, was casting surreptitious glances at his wristwatch, she said pointedly to Adam, forcing herself to meet his regard impersonally, 'It's a working day tomorrow and we both know about surgeons' early starts. Please don't feel you have to wait until I'm finished.'

'There's no hurry.' She sensed that inwardly he was laughing at her. 'For you, I've allocated all night.'

'In that case, I'll leave the two of you to it.' Duncan met her embarrassed look calmly as the two men stood and shook hands. 'Adam, a pleasure. It's rare that we have the opportunity to communicate with our colleagues outside our own narrow field and I've enjoyed hearing a fresh voice tonight. I hope we can do this again soon.'

'I'd like that,' the surgeon replied, both his words and the easy self-assurance behind the gaze which brushed Susan's face making her teeth grit.

'Duncan, there's no need for you to go,' she said urgently. 'I'm only going to be a few minutes. We can walk over to the cars together.'

'No, Susan.' Duncan rejected the offer with barely a glance in her direction, his attention concentrated instead on Adam as the men completed their farewells. 'Adam will look after you.'

Adam wouldn't be given the chance, she thought, feeling herself beginning to become panicky. 'Your sister was right,' she hissed, seconds later once Duncan had gone, leaving them alone. 'You're a rat.'

'So stop fighting me,' he said softly, his expression remaining infuriatingly calm in response to the anger she wasn't bothering to conceal. 'Stop fighting and I'll be nice.'

'No, thank you.' She pushed her glasses higher on her nose, the better to glare at him. 'You are the most impolite, discourteous and arrogant man I have ever met. How dare you…fondle me like that in front of Duncan?'

'Next time I'll be more circumspect,' he promised.

'There isn't going to be a next time,' she said tightly. 'And if there is then you can count me out. You two can form your own mutual admiration society.'

'What were you expecting?' Putting her now empty coffee cup away from her, he took her hand and tugged her gently but determinedly out of the booth. 'Pistols at dawn?'

'That would have been nice.'

'Two years, Susan.' He took her coat from the waiter and held it for her, his hands taking her shoulders briefly and holding her still once she'd shrugged it on. 'Something would have happened by now if it was going to.'

'You don't know anything about either of us,' she muttered fiercely, keeping her head lowered. 'You don't understand. Duncan and I are very suited. He's…he's everything I want in a man. Just because—'

She broke off, realising how unwise it would be to continue, and felt relieved when after a brief hesitation he released her shoulders so that she could turn towards the door.

Her relief was short-lived. He took her hand as they waited for the traffic to clear before crossing the road, and she decided it was easier simply to let him get away with it than to try and fight him. 'Just because you don't feel any desire to share your bed with him?' he said quietly.

Susan didn't look at him. 'He's never asked me to.'

'Which means?'

'No more than that he's a gentleman.'

The area they were in was well lit by streetlamps and a quick glance up at his face told her that he was unimpressed by that assessment but he seemed to have elected not to push her on it. They walked in what to her felt like an increasingly awkward silence across to the medical school's grounds and along the tree-lined main road towards the area where she'd left her car.

'The nurses tell me Tony's move to Churchill went uneventfully,' she said finally. 'He's started the fluoxetine. That's the antidepressant,' she added quickly, realising that he might not know that. 'I'll review his progress on Monday afternoon.' When the only response to that was a dry look she continued, 'How is his…um, pelvis going? Any problems on that front?'

'No.'

'So everything's all right with his traction then?'

The hand holding hers tightened. 'Why do I make you so nervous?'

'Because you won't take no for an answer.' Her tone was sharp since it seemed an observation that was entirely self-evident. 'You'd make any woman nervous. I've never met anybody so single-minded. I don't want to have anything to do with you, Adam Hargraves. If you think I didn't keep pushing your hand away tonight because I liked what you were doing then you're very wrong. I just didn't want to embarrass Duncan. You're wasting your time coming with me now or any time. I'm not going to invite you home with me.'

They were close to her car now and she pulled her hand away fiercely and groped awkwardly in her bag for her keys. 'Thank you, but here we are. I can manage the rest of the way on my own now.'

When he still didn't say anything she walked quickly around to the driver's door of her little car, fumbled with her keys and finally unlocked the vehicle. 'I don't suppose we'll be meeting socially again,' she said quickly, opening the door and throwing her bag onto the empty passenger's seat. 'I'll liaise with your registrar about Tony. Goodbye.'

'Coward.'

She was about to climb into the car but that single soft word was enough to draw her slowly straight again. 'Once again you're wrong—' she began primly, intending to make a fluent and logical little speech about how his opinion of himself and his attractions was vastly out of sync with her own thoughts on the matter, but he moved so deliberately and so quickly that she was caught unawares as he tugged her away from the vehicle, closed her door then backed her against it.

Somehow, confused, she lost track of things then but what she did know—and the knowledge astounded her—was that it was she who kissed him first, not the other way around, and that now, unlike the night she'd met him, she had no thought of fighting him.

They kissed once, twice, small…testing kisses. Again, another one, pulling back each time so she stared up at him, her eyes painfully wide as she tried to read his heavy regard, her mind numb. But then, as if he'd lost patience with that, strong hands went behind her, gathered in her coat hard so that she could feel them curling through the fabric into her skin and lifted her forward and hard against him. Abruptly he turned hungry and her pulse soared and she realised that, far from being an unwilling supplicant, her desire incredibly and inexplicably suddenly matched the urgency she could sense in him.

How long they stood like that, she had no idea, only that when they finally drew apart her hair was loose from where his hands had roamed her, her mouth was bare and sore and her body felt heated and damp beneath the uncomfortable weight of her clothes.

'Th-this is a terrible mistake,' she stammered breathlessly. It came out hoarse. 'Something's gone wrong in my…in my…well, something's just gone wrong.'

'Don't think so much,' he said roughly. He reached for her again but this time she ducked away under his arms.

She moved quickly to put the width of her car between them, calming a little when he didn't follow. 'No,' she said strongly. 'I mean it.'

When he didn't move, but instead slid his fists into his pockets and stood regarding her with a brooding intensity that made her pulse start to skip again, she stumbled out an explanation.

'I didn't mean to… I realise I've just… I didn't mean that to happen.' She felt stupid, clumsy, all her words coming only with difficulty. 'I don't even understand why it keeps happening unless it's something to do with how long… I mean, I wish that you could see that I'm not responding to you as a person but probably I'd do the same to any… Look, it's just not going to work,' she finished lamely.

'Susan,' he said heavily. 'Are you trying to tell me you don't like me touching you?'

'No,' she admitted, knowing that he knew better than that. 'But I didn't like it in any deep, emotional way. Just…on a superficial, physical level.'

'Physical's fine.'

'Not for me,' she said abruptly, flushing again. She found herself wringing her hands. 'In many ways the way you can make me feel is very…interesting. It's just that I think it's important that we both take a rational look at things here. We're completely unsuited—'

'That doesn't mean we can't have good sex.'

'To me that's exactly what it means,' she insisted, appalled. 'Adam, I don't want to hurt your feelings—'

'Hurt them.'

Blinking at the harshness of his tone, she recoiled a little. 'I... no...'

'Hurt them.'

She hesitated but his expression told her that without honesty things would only get worse. 'I'm sure that under this...pushy surface you're a very nice man,' she said quickly, almost breathlessly in her haste to get the words out. 'And I know from what I've overheard on the wards that you're very good at your job and well respected. But I'm not looking for a casual relationship. Even if I was, you still wouldn't be the...sort of man I'd be looking for. I want to find someone more...' She hesitated. 'No, I mean *less*, less...physical.'

'Less physical?'

'More intellectual,' she said wearily.

'*Intellectual?*'

To her relief he seemed more puzzled than offended, but still, feeling ashamed, she hung her head. 'You don't have to tell me that makes me sound like the most horrible sort of snob,' she mumbled, 'because I already feel terrible about it, but I'm just trying to be as honest as I can be. I'm a psychiatrist. I've analysed myself and I know that I understand myself completely. The only way I'll ever be able to have a satisfying relationship physically is if I first find my...my...'

'Intellectual equal?'

'Oh, no, not that, not an equal or a superior, simply a soul mate,' she said quickly, lifting her head, guessing from his shadowed expression that her explanation must sound terribly inadequate. 'Someone with whom I *connect* on a mental level. Someone with whom I can imagine spending the rest of my life simply enjoying our conversation.'

'Conversation?' he echoed.

'Mmm.' She wrung her hands and flushed, again, this time at his scepticism.

'Conversation,' he repeated heavily.

Susan nodded. 'I'm not a *physical* person,' she explained. 'I'm not the sort of person who will ever relax enough with a man to find sexual pleasure in his arms without first forming a strong intellectual bond with him.'

'You won't find sexual pleasure…?' She heard him sigh. 'Susan, you can't know that.'

'But I do.'

'You're a virgin.'

'And a psychiatrist,' she said quietly. 'I understand myself.'

'Take care not to grow over-confident,' he replied, equally quietly. 'You understand less than you think you do.'

It seemed that was all he had to say on the subject because he opened the driver's door of her car and moved away far enough for her to feel it was safe to walk warily around and climb inside.

'I'm glad we've had this little chat,' she told him, wishing that the words had come out a little more steadily. 'I feel as if we've cleared the air. I'm sorry if I've offended you, Adam, but at least we both know now exactly where we stand.'

Feeling better, she closed the door, then wound down her window. 'We may meet on work matters but I don't expect we'll be seeing each other on a personal level any more. I wish you well, Adam. I'm sure one day you'll find the right woman for you.'

Seeing how his expression darkened at that, Susan started her car hurriedly. 'Well, then…goodbye.' She drove off jerkily.

CHAPTER SIX

ADAM was scheduled for Orthopaedic Outpatients on Friday morning and after his ward round he and his registrar went directly to clinic. They used ten rooms in the outpatients suite, four for him so that he could see a number of people in quick succession without waiting each time for them to undress where required, two for Christopher, one for each of his two SHOs, one for his research registrar and one central room to be used as their meeting room for them to liaise and inspect the notes and X-rays they needed for the clinic.

They worked fast because they had to. Cuts to the casualty department's budget meant that follow up of routine orthopaedic injuries there had been abandoned, forcing more cases onto his already crowded list.

Demand for his clinic now was so high that just to keep up with the scheduled appointments—leaving aside emergencies, which were added without appointments—they had to see over eighty patients an hour. Because of the relative inexperience of his more junior staff, either he or Christopher had to see the bulk of those cases.

The system worked. Just. But what they didn't need, in the middle of the morning's chaos, was a crisis on one of the wards.

'It's about Tony,' Christopher told him apologetically after taking an urgent bleep from Denise, one of Adam's house officers. 'There was some problem with the special nursing thing this morning and he was left alone. He broke a glass and used it to slash one of his wrists. He's threat-

106

ening the staff with the glass now and he won't let any of them near him to see the wound. Security hasn't been able to get to him. He looks all right but he's still bleeding.'

'Tell Denise I'm on my way.' His face tightening, Adam dropped the notes he'd been working through and collected his white coat from where he'd left it behind the door. By sheer weight of authority he calculated that he had more chance of getting through to the man than his juniors—he was also bigger than any of them if force was needed to disarm Tony. 'Carry on here,' he told Christopher. 'Just arrange knee views on the man in room three who's been referred with left hip pain. Mrs Martin in two needs to go onto my semi-urgent list for a left total hip and the child in four should stay here for me to examine when I get back.'

He called out for the clinic's charge nurse. 'Linda, if the delay gets longer than forty minutes make some sort of announcement to warn everyone. Chris, bleep Susan Wheelan. If she's around see if she can meet me up on the ward.'

His patient, bedclothes around his left arm red with blood, face pale but determined, made a fairly pathetic picture despite managing to hold half a ward of nurses as well as three junior doctors and two security officers at bay with a few shards of broken glass in one outstretched, trembling hand.

'Don't be an idiot,' Adam said tersely, the thought of the patients he was keeping waiting leaving him in no mood for tiptoeing around Tony's delicate mental balance. Unceremoniously he strode directly to the younger man, immobilised his wrist and disarmed him.

He dumped the broken glass into a disposable bucket one of the nurses held out for him, took the gloves his house officer offered him, pulled them on and examined his patient's injured wrist. 'Superficial,' he declared, extending Tony's arm so that Denise could inspect it. 'No arterial, tendon or nerve damage. You'll get away with a clean, some Steri-strips and a solid bandage.'

Questions about the lack of a psychiatric nurse and about how Tony had got hold of the glass in the first place wouldn't help, he decided, guessing from the stricken faces of the doctors and nurses around him that such an error would never recur. 'No one,' he told Tony, turning his grim attention finally to his patient's pinched face, 'threatens or harms the staff on my ward. Understand?'

The younger man looked away. 'They should have left me alone,' he mumbled.

'That isn't going to happen,' Adam ruled. 'You're not going to be left alone again for one minute. Whether you like it or not you're leaving my ward alive and intact. I didn't spend four hours in an operating theatre joining your pelvis together just to let you kill yourself before you're out of my care. Lie there, keep quiet and let Denise clean up your arm.'

He turned away from the bed, leaving his house officer with Tony's injured wrist, and waved the rest of the staff— except for the ward's charge nurse—away. 'Have we got anyone to sit with him?'

'I'll stay with him until the psych nurse gets here,' she promised. 'We had a call a few minutes ago to say he was running late this morning. I'm sorry, Adam. There was an agency nurse covering him overnight and I didn't realise she'd gone off duty without waiting to hand over to the psych cover. If I had, I'd have assigned one of the ward nurses to stand in.'

'I'm sure it won't happen again.' Adam lifted his arm wearily to stop her. 'We need something to keep things calm for a while. Get me two point five of haloperidol to start.'

'No sedation.'

Susan's soft voice brought his head up and his senses abruptly alert. His eyes narrowing and moving so she was shielded from Tony's view, he said heavily, 'He slashed his wrist.'

'So I hear,' she said, her tone equally quiet. 'It's all right. I'm sorry there was a breakdown in our system this morning but I'll take charge now. When your house officer's finished with his injuries I'll assess him. Looking at him now, I don't believe there's any need to sedate him.'

Accepting her superior expertise in matters of his patient's psyche, Adam agreed to leave it to her judgement. 'I have to get back to Outpatients. If you get a chance when you're finished here bleep me—otherwise I'll call you later. Either way, we need to discuss this.'

'Of course.'

The formal, businesslike nature of their discussion, necessitated by the presence of the charge nurse beside them, didn't make it seem any less frustrating to Adam when invariably the only interaction he found himself contemplating when he considered the psychiatrist was a far more intimate one.

He wasn't used to having to work at keeping his mind on his job. He was even less used to having to work at seduction.

Susan was unlike any woman he'd ever known. He was used to open, confident lovers—women who acknowledged and enjoyed their sexuality—but she was guarded and tightly cautious. Too analytical to trust her body's instincts, she protected herself with veils of words.

He understood now that that difference meant that his mistake had been in being too direct and unambiguous in his expression of his desire. Deception was beyond him but he recognised that he had to learn to adjust himself to her. He had to learn fast. The acknowledgement that in three days what had started out as a prickling of uncomplicated desire had evolved into an obsession that kept him restless by night and distracted by day didn't come easily to him, but his reaction to her forced him to accept it.

He didn't know if it was an indication of how long he'd gone without sex, or simply that she was the only woman he'd wanted who'd not come easily to him, but the way he felt now he'd never wanted anything or anyone so badly.

Susan was right when she said they had little in common but that didn't change anything for him. He had to get his life and his work and his head back together again. He knew enough about himself to know that for that to happen he had to have her.

'I'll leave things in your capable hands,' he said evenly, unable, despite knowing from her muddled little speeches the night before that she might not appreciate the gesture, to stop his eyes straying momentarily to the enticingly soft curve of her mouth.

His lapse was momentary, but when he lifted his gaze higher, irritated with himself for his weakness, the sudden lowering of her thick lashes together with the blush of colour that rose to stain her pale cheeks reassured him that, far from being angered by his regard, she was as disturbed by his nearness as he was by hers.

Which offered some compensation for the discomfort of his own thoughts. Not that he wasn't finding the situation totally without…pleasure, he conceded. For despite his frustration the experience of the chase was novel enough to intrigue him, even if he found it far less physically…comfortable than he'd have preferred.

'I'll hear from you soon,' he told her neutrally, aware, again, of the others around them. 'About Tony.'

Taking care not to alarm her anew by allowing their arms to touch as he moved past her towards the door, he merely nodded a farewell. 'Denise, are you all right with that?'

'Fine, thanks.' His house officer answered promptly, lifting her head from where she'd been bent over Tony's arm. 'Almost finished.'

His juniors had done well, keeping up with the clinic, and by one-thirty, only thirty minutes later than scheduled, they'd almost cleared the waiting room.

'Grab some lunch while you've got the chance,' he advised Christopher when the charge nurse told him there were only three people left to see. Because they were scheduled for surgical teaching sessions during that lunch interval, the SHOs and his research registrar had already gone. 'I'll finish things here and meet you in Theatre at two.'

The younger doctor nodded his thanks and gathered up the last of his notes. 'Should I check Tony first?'

'Not now.' One of the staff nurses had taken a telephone message from Susan when Adam had been tied up, moulding a plaster and unable to answer his bleep, to say that he should call her when he was free and that it was regarding their mutual patient. 'Lunch,' he told his registrar. 'We'd have heard if he hadn't settled by now.'

He finished seeing his last set of patients, dictated brief letters for his secretary to type up and send to their GPs concerning the consultations, then bleeped Susan.

He kept his tone deliberately brisk. 'Adam Hargraves here, Susan, returning your call. How's Tony?'

'He's calm now.' He thought she sounded cautious. 'He'll be all right tonight and I've made sure there's good psychiatric cover for the weekend. Adam, I'd like to apologise again for the slip-up—'

'It wasn't your fault,' he said, cutting her off. 'Having happened once, I'm sure we've all learned enough for it not to happen again.'

'Thank you for seeing it that way,' she answered. 'And I promise you it definitely won't. Happen again, that is.'

'Good.' He found himself reluctant to break the contact. 'Is there anything else I should know about him?'

'I don't think so.' But she sounded unsure and a few moments later rushed on, 'Oh, no, there is one other thing I wanted to ask you about. I've managed to persuade Tony's family to come in tonight for a family meeting. I'll be there, as well as a nurse from each team and his social worker. They were very reluctant to meet me and I'm sure there's something going on within the family that I don't understand yet. Tony's agreed to the meeting but he hasn't decided whether he wants to be involved or not. As well as seeing how they interact, it'll be a chance to make sure that everyone's well informed.

'Would your registrar or house officer be free to attend to explain things from the orthopaedic perspective? Or perhaps you, if they're not? Tony's father works full time and aside from that he and his brother have both been very hard to pin down. I could only organise the meeting for after hours. Is seven too late?'

'It is for my juniors when we're not on call,' he said heavily, registering the fact that he'd been her final choice of doctor. Unless junior doctors were on call for the night, in which case they worked through until the following evening, they were scheduled to finish at five.

In practice he knew his own staff rarely left before six and Christopher would stay on if he asked him to, but he didn't feel it was fair to do that—especially as they were all on call from nine the following morning for the entire weekend.

'I'm happy to come myself,' he told her, 'but I've an appointment which means I'll need to leave by seven-thirty.'

She came back with, 'Seven-thirty's fine.' He thought she sounded nervous again. 'That'll be a great help. Thank you. We're meeting in the seminar room beneath Churchill by your trauma unit.'

He arrived just before seven, but although Susan was waiting with three casually dressed young people—he assumed they must be the social worker and the psychiatric nurses—neither Tony nor his family were present.

'Tony's decided not to join us,' Susan explained. 'It's not a good sign, but not unexpected. I'm sorry, but the others seem to be running a little late. Adam, this is John Mills and Natalie Patel, two of our nurses from the psychiatric side. And this is Reece Wilson, Tony's social worker.'

He exchanged nods of acknowledgement with the three. 'I'll be across in the trauma unit when the others arrive,' he said neutrally, taking care to confine his attention to her face.

There were X-rays he wanted to check, but his main reason for not staying was that the red jacket Susan had been wearing earlier was slung across the back of her chair and the fitted blouse she now displayed outlined the lifting curve of her breasts far too closely for his peace of mind.

As he wasn't confident that irritation at himself for reacting like a sex-obsessed adolescent would stop him behaving like one, it seemed wise to avoid giving himself the opportunity. 'Call out when you're ready to start.'

The others arrived and Susan started the meeting about ten minutes later. She welcomed Tony's relatives and in-

troduced everyone in the room by first names only, and
Adam's mouth quirked as he registered the difference between the psychiatric and surgical services. In twelve years
in orthopaedics he couldn't remember ever having been
introduced by his first name before.

She made a quick reference to the fact that Tony had
been calm since the morning's episode, from which Adam
deduced that she'd told his family what had happened, then
she explained that he had to leave early. 'So, Adam, perhaps we could start with you outlining Tony's injuries and
what you've done.'

He explained about his patient's fractured pelvis and
legs and his arm and briefly about the surgery he'd performed to stabilise his bones. 'It's difficult to predict how
long he'll need to be on bed rest,' he explained. 'At this
stage I'd anticipate twelve weeks, depending on how well
the bones at the back of his pelvis knit, but until we see
some healing reaction in his X-rays I can't give you any
firmer idea.'

'In some ways I understand why he might want to...end
it all.' Tony's sister's puffy eyes suggested she'd been cry-
ing. 'I'd feel the same if I thought I was never going to
walk again.'

Adam frowned, puzzled by that. 'But he will,' he said
firmly. 'He will walk. There's no evidence of nerve damage and his spinal cord is unaffected. There's a possibility
he may end up with a limp favouring his left side and he
may have some residual pain in the area but there's still a
good chance he'll be symptom-free.'

'Have you told Tony that?' his father demanded, but
behind his belligerent tone Adam thought that he, too,
looked confused. 'Has anyone bothered to tell him? Carla's
just been in to see him. He didn't say much, but from what

he let slip it's pretty obvious he's expecting to end up in a wheelchair.'

'There's never been any doubt that he'd walk,' Adam reiterated. 'His injuries don't warrant any concern in that direction.'

'But all those wires,' his sister protested. 'And the bolts and that triangle thing sticking out of his bones. He can't move, can he?'

'The devices you see aren't because he can't move. We're simply using them to hold his pelvis and legs in the right position to encourage good healing.' Adam frowned. 'Tony knows that. He's been kept fully informed.'

Adam saw that they still looked hostile but he was at a loss to think of anything to say that might convince them.

Clearly Susan agreed with his assessment because she said quietly, 'Tony's depression makes it hard for him to believe in good things. At this stage he sees only the pessimistic side of life. As his mood improves you'll find he becomes more positive about his future. And obviously his communication with you isn't ideal at present.'

'When you say it's difficult to say how long he'll be in that stuff.' Tony's brother, silent until now, was staring at Adam. 'When you say that, do you mean he could be in it for much longer than you might think?'

'It's possible,' Adam conceded. 'At present twelve weeks would be my upper estimate but it's possible his pelvis will take longer to heal.'

'How much longer?'

'Theoretically…any amount of time,' Adam said slowly, mystified by their continuing doubt. 'Occasionally the bones don't join on their own, in which case we have to look at intervening surgically again. Bone transplants, further pinning or another plate—that sort of thing. But that's theoretical for now. I've seen no indication that your brother's fractures are going to mend any way other than normally.'

There was a brief, charged silence then Susan asked quietly, 'Is there a reason you're having trouble dealing with Tony's time here in hospital?'

'The wife died in here,' Tony's father said finally, slowly, as if the fact had been drawn painfully from him. 'She slipped on a bit of wet floor and hurt her hip. I brought her in to Casualty and they made her stay in for X-rays. Three weeks later she was dead.

'The nurse in Casualty told us that she'd broken her leg and that she needed an operation, but then the doctor said there wasn't going to be any operation. The next day they told us that it wasn't just a broken leg but a cancer in the bone. From the lung, they told us. It had spread to her leg. Then they stuck needles and tubes into her and told us that it wasn't coming from the lung at all but from her breast.'

Both he and his daughter had started weeping now, and while Adam understood the reason for their grief he didn't intuitively know what he should do. Fortunately the other staff clearly didn't share his inadequacy because the psychiatric nurses moved immediately to put comforting arms around Tony's sister and father.

'They said radiation would help,' Tony's father said unevenly. 'But it didn't. It made her sick and it didn't make any difference to the cancer. We wanted her at home but they kept her in here doing tests. We couldn't understand why they wanted to do tests when they knew there was nothing more they could do. In three weeks she wasted away to nothing. They let her die in here.'

'I'm very sorry you lost someone so dear to you so suddenly like that,' Susan said quietly. 'We all know that there's nothing I can say that can possibly change how you feel or make anything any better, but please believe that you have our deepest sympathy.'

'You'll understand why we…why John and me haven't been able to bring ourselves in to visit Tony,' the older man said roughly. 'They brought her to his ward first before she got transferred over to the cancer ward. We can't come in here without remembering how she suffered those last days.'

'I could arrange for Tony to be transferred to Chamberlain Ward two floors down,' Adam offered, relieved to be able to do something practical for them. Chamberlain was primarily a plastic surgery ward but it had six orthopaedic beds and it wouldn't be difficult to organise a swap with one of his other patients. 'Would that help make it a little easier to come in?'

Tony's father straightened a little at that, as if the idea interested him, but, sending Adam a clear look that he was unable to decipher, Susan intervened. 'I think that that's an interesting suggestion and certainly it provides a short-term solution because Tony needs you all at this time.'

She looked at Tony's father. 'But, Martin, would moving Tony really help or am I right to feel that the problem goes deeper than that? Will moving him to another ward make it any easier for you to come to the hospital? Would moving him to another hospital make it easier for you to come and spend time with your son when he's sick?'

'He doesn't want to see us.' Tony's brother answered instead. 'He said as much to Carla. He wants to be left in peace.'

'If he's aware of how difficult it is for you to come to the ward, he may be trying to spare your feelings,' Susan said gently. 'Underneath the bravado and sadness, Tony's a very sensitive young man.'

'Used to be,' his father observed, 'as a lad. Before his

mother died. Before he went wild. Before the drugs and the bikes. He's changed now.'

'It's you that's changed.' Tony's sister had tears running down his face. 'Not Tony. You've been too hard on him. Since Mum…you've been too hard on all of us.'

Beside Adam, Tony's brother curled up, dropping his head onto his knees and wrapping his arms around them.

Freely admitting that, despite his concern for the family, he was completely out of his depth, Adam slid along to the next seat beside him to allow room for Susan to slip in next to the man and comfort him.

'Adam, you go,' the psychiatrist murmured. 'You've got your meeting. We'll finish here.'

Not arguing, he made for the door, relieved to be able to leave the rest of the session in her hands. The family was too distraught to even realise that he was leaving and he slipped out, quietly pulling the door closed behind him.

Margaret, although he was sure she should have left hours ago, was still on duty in the trauma unit when he came onto the ward. She scanned his face and smiled. 'Poor man,' she teased, clearly having interpreted his expression correctly. 'Was the psych meeting too harrowing for you?'

'Some of us were just meant to be surgeons,' Adam admitted heavily, going directly to the X-ray board to check the set of films he'd ordered before the meeting. 'That position's good now,' he declared, referring to an adjustment they'd made earlier in the traction on the patient in bed two, an admission from the day before with multiple injuries following a head-on car smash in Commercial Road. He'd been transferred to them from out of their own area because the Royal London's ICU and trauma unit were both full. He'd seemed stable on admission but they'd been having difficulty ventilating him for much of that afternoon. 'How's his chest?'

'Early ARDS, as we assumed,' Lawrence told him, his appearance from the side-passage to his office reminding Adam that his brother-in-law would be on call for the night until Adam took over at eight the next morning. 'I've pushed his oxygen up and we're keeping a close eye on him, but he's stable at present,' he continued, referring to part of the management for ARDS, or adult respiratory distress syndrome, a potentially lethal lung complication which they sometimes saw in patients with multi-system injuries. 'Thought you had a meeting tonight?'

'I'm on my way.' The university's research-funding committee was meeting at eight to discuss the following year's grants, and since his own work accounted for a large piece of the orthopaedic department's budget he'd agreed to brief the committee on their work. 'I'll be in at eight tomorrow.'

But Lawrence came after him. 'Adam, what about tomorrow night? Barbara said to remind you about dinner.'

After giving the still-closed door of the seminar room a wary glance on his way past, Adam sent the other man an exasperated look. 'Larry, I've already told Babs no. The fact that she's cluttered up my machines with insistent messages hasn't changed my mind.'

'You must know Barbara would never take any notice of a little thing like your refusal,' Lawrence protested. 'Besides, it's a party. She's got lots of people coming so it won't matter if you slip out early.'

Adam sent him an old-fashioned look. 'You're not fooling anyone, Larry.'

'OK, OK.' The other man looked sheepish. 'Yes, she's got someone coming especially for you to meet. You can't not come. It's all arranged.'

Adam closed his eyes briefly, remembering when he'd last heard similar words. At the stairwell he swung around. 'Let me guess,' he said wearily. 'She's a sports teacher.'

Lawrence looked mildly surprised. 'Yes,' he admitted gingerly. 'But she's gorgeous,' he continued more enthusiastically. 'I promise.'

'I know she's gorgeous because I've seen her photograph. But I also know that I told Babs I wasn't interested. I told her to introduce her to Chris McInnes.'

'Barbara wouldn't have because she's absolutely convinced this one is perfect for you,' the anaesthetist countered.

'Larry—'

'She's doing Thai curries.'

'Tempting,' Adam conceded, 'but not enough. Barbara's just going to have to apologise to the teacher. I'm not interested. Besides, I'm on call.'

'That doesn't mean you won't be free tomorrow night. Christopher's experienced enough not to need to call you in for much.'

'Even if I'm not needed in Theatre, I'll be in working,' Adam countered. 'My paperwork's backed up.' His mouth tightened as he contemplated his brother-in-law's reaction if he explained that his concentration had been impaired that week because he'd spent valuable working hours brooding about how best to seduce a reluctant psychiatrist. 'There's more than enough to get through in the lab to keep me busy all weekend.'

'Remember Susan?'

Adam's eyes narrowed on the anaesthetist's smugly knowing expression. 'Vaguely.'

'Her sister and brother-in-law are coming. Annabel and Mike from the other night.' Lawrence looked pleased with himself. 'Barbara's invited them.'

'And Susan?'

'Are you kidding?' He rolled his eyes. 'Barbara would eat razor blades rather than let you anywhere near her. No. Not a chance. She won't be there. But still…Annabel seemed keen on the idea of you two getting together. She might have some useful…suggestions.'

Adam frowned. 'Tell Barbara I'll come,' he said heavily, 'if I'm not caught up on call and on condition that I invite two more guests.' He'd heard enough complaints from Christopher about the lamentable state of both his registrar's finances and sex life to assume he wouldn't turn down a free dinner and the chance of a blind date with a beautiful teacher. 'Think she'll buy it?'

'To get you and the teacher together she'd take another dozen,' Lawrence said cheerfully, calling after him as Adam started down the stairs. 'So, who are this mysterious couple?'

'I'm late,' Adam called back from the floor below. 'Can't stop.'

CHAPTER SEVEN

ON CALL for St Martin's for the weekend, Susan went into the hospital first thing Saturday morning to meet up with the on-call registrar and to check the psychiatric wards.

'Quiet,' Roy, the nurse in charge of the unit told her on Winchester Ward. 'We've twelve out on weekend leave and peace and harmony reigns. Susan, baby, any news on Mrs Bibby going home?'

'I'm seeing her landlord at eleven-thirty,' Susan said wearily. She'd meant to meet him the night before but the session with Tony's family had lasted far longer than she'd anticipated and she'd had to miss the appointment. 'I'm not hopeful. He didn't sound very interested when I spoke to him on the telephone.'

She peered out of the office into the day-room, which was empty apart from two of her psycho-geriatric patients who were smoking and reading newspapers in one corner. 'I'll go up and see Tony on Churchill,' she told her registrar who was standing beside her and the charge nurse. 'There's no point in you seeing him since the ward calls me directly with problems anyway. Anything happening in Casualty?'

'Nothing I've been told about and I've had no GP calls,' the younger doctor said. He held up crossed fingers. 'All signs good for a quiet weekend.'

'We've had a message to say Tony's been moved from Churchill to Chamberlain,' Roy told her as she moved to leave the office.

'Already?' Susan lifted her brows, impressed by the

speed with which Adam Hargraves had managed that. At nine the night before her patient had still been on Churchill and the nurses hadn't thought there'd be any chance of him making the move until after the weekend. 'Great. Any problems reported overnight with him?'

'All's sweet,' Roy reassured her. 'The orthopaedic nurse who covered last night said he slept. This morning he's talked a bit about the work he used to do. The way I hear it, that's the first time he's offered anything spontaneously. Groovy, hmm?'

'It is,' Susan agreed, pleased at the improvement. When one talked with Tony it tended to be very much a question-and-answer session, with long gaps before he said anything at all.

'I hear a lot of heavy grief went down at the family session last night.'

'There's unresolved grief and anger about the way Tony's mother died,' she agreed. 'It seems to be the pivotal point in the breakdown of Tony's relationship with his family but I still don't feel that I understand why. His father's not ready for any sort of reconciliation but his brother and sister seem more willing. His sister talked about coming in to see him again today, which is why I'm pleased they've managed to move him so quickly. I've scheduled another counselling session for the family for Monday night. But, given how upset they were last night, though, there's no guarantee they'll turn up.'

'Where's Tony coming from on this?'

'He seems indifferent.' On her way out of the door, Susan shrugged. 'I still think it's worth persisting. We're not going to create the perfect family or anything, but if they can work through whatever conflict's behind their problems Tony might not be so susceptible to these bouts of depression.'

Tony seemed, she thought, after spending a few minutes with him, marginally less withdrawn that morning.

'And he even managed a whole Weetabix.' Sally, the psychiatric nurse supervising him for the morning, rolled expressive eyes. 'What an exciting shift this is turning out to be.'

Susan laughed. 'Hopefully not as exciting as yesterday,' she said lightly. 'Tony, how's your wrist?'

'All right.' He slowly lifted both arms so she could see that both his hands had now been bound, mitten-like. 'Mr Hargraves made them wrap me up like this last night.'

'He's not taking any chances,' Susan said. 'You heard him. He doesn't want you topping yourself before whatever brilliant repair he's done to your pelvis gets a chance to be used.'

'They come off for eating,' Sally explained.

'He says I've got to wear them all weekend,' Tony told her.

'He's the boss,' Susan said evenly. She didn't mind about the mittens. At least, not in the short term. There was a small trade off in that it removed from Tony the responsibility for his own behaviour, but the benefit was that they also provided tangible and obvious proof that there was someone who cared that he stayed alive and unharmed.

Even if it was only to protect the metal in his pelvis, she conceded, amused by the lengths to which Adam was prepared to go to ensure that his work didn't go unappreciated.

'I'm having another meeting with your father and Carla and John on Monday night,' she told him. 'It's up to you, but you might find it useful to come along.'

Her patient's face closed. He looked away from her without saying anything.

'Think about it,' she said neutrally. Nodding to Sally, she left the room.

She'd intended to leave discussion of the session the night before with Adam Hargraves until after the weekend, but when she emerged onto the ward she saw that he was taking a ward round in the next cubicle and she froze, startled by seeing him when she hadn't anticipated it.

He looked up from his discussion with his registrar and a nurse, and caught her eye briefly. Realising that to escape now would merely make her appear skittish and silly, she walked as calmly as she could manage across the corridor to the nurses' station and waited for him, trying to ignore the involuntary quickening of her pulse which his proximity invariably provoked.

'Try using that bar there, Andrew.' From where she was waiting she couldn't help but overhear their round and she was especially sensitive to Adam's low tones.

She saw their pale-looking patient haul himself slowly up an inch, using what looked like a metal triangle suspended on a chain from the ward's ceiling. Like a caricature of a figure in a holiday insurance advertisement, the young man seemed to have every limb—bar the one he was using to support himself—in traction or casts. Both his chest and his head were heavily encased in bandages, and what she could see of his abdomen and worried-looking face appeared scarred by grazes and cuts.

To her less-than-practised eyes the only part of the lad that didn't appear obviously injured was his back, and it was this that Adam Hargraves and his registrar were crouching to examine.

'Tell me if there's pain when I do this,' the surgeon instructed.

Susan couldn't see what it was he did but she saw his

patient's mouth open and heard him grunt. 'Pain,' he gasped.

'Compression L2,' Adam ruled, and Susan knew that that meant he'd diagnosed a fracture of one of the vertebrae in the young man's lower spine. 'He'll need another set of films,' he told his registrar. 'Get base of skull views, check his feet and request a CT.'

Christopher, Adam's registrar, hurried out to go to the computer at the main desk, nodding acknowledgement as he passed Susan. 'He won't be long,' he told her quickly. 'This is the last patient we've been asked to see here. How's Tony?'

'Brighter this morning,' Susan said absently, impressed by the thoroughness with which his boss was undertaking a neurological exam, particularly given the limitations posed by his patient being in plaster and traction.

'What happened to him?'

Christopher glanced up from the screen as he tapped in some details. 'Andrew? Drunken fall through a second-floor glass door. He's been complaining of abdominal and back pain overnight but the team who admitted him didn't pick up the compression fracture.'

She tried to keep her attention on the registrar but she couldn't stop her gaze drifting back to Adam again. 'Are you on call this weekend?'

'For orthopaedics,' Christopher confirmed, sounding as if he was still tapping at the keys. 'Every second weekend on we cover plastics as well but thankfully this isn't it.'

'Is it too busy with plastics?'

'Too busy when there's a party to go to.' The younger man grinned at her. 'The boss has wangled me an invite to a free dinner tonight,' he explained. 'If it's quiet enough here for the SHO to handle things, I'll be able to go.'

Adam had moved on to examining their patient's distended-looking abdomen, and Susan found herself mesmerised by the careful movements of his hands as he probed each quadrant in turn. 'Aren't you supposed to stay on site?'

'All surgical SHOs here are resident, meaning the registrars can be on call from home.' He tapped one more key on the computer then slid his chair back and left it. 'Or,' he said lightly, darting past her, 'from a party.'

'X-rays ordered,' she heard him say to Adam. 'I've put them as urgent so he should be taken down within fifteen minutes. Unless there's any neurological problem, we won't get a CT before Monday.'

His consultant looked up from where he was listening to their patient's abdomen with a stethoscope and nodded. 'Neurologically, no apparent impairment,' he told him, 'but he's got an ileus. There're no bowel sounds. Nil by mouth, IV fluids and a nasogastric tube on continuous suction. Plain films of his abdomen if there's no improvement within twenty-four hours.'

He turned back to his patient. 'Nothing more to eat or drink, Andrew. Your stomach's gone on strike in protest at the damage to your back. It'll settle down in a day or two, but in the meantime we'll give you fluids through a drip. The nurses will bring injections for the pain. The injury to your back will be treated with bed rest for a few days then physiotherapy to help you with movement again.'

From where Susan was standing, the surgeon's smile looked sympathetic. 'That just about covers every part of your body,' he said evenly. 'Anything you need to know?'

'Will I...? I'm a bit worried about my girlfriend,' the young man said quietly. Susan saw him look around worriedly and she lowered her eyes so he wouldn't realise that anyone else could hear him. 'I don't remember much of what they said when they brought me in and I didn't know who to ask. I was wondering…with all the pain and everything, is everything down there…?'

'If you're talking about sex then everything's fine in that area,' Adam said calmly. Glancing up, Susan saw that he'd taken his patient's concern seriously. 'In fact, I'd say that area's the only part of you that's escaped unscathed.'

'Great.' Susan smiled at the boy's grin. 'Great. Fantastic. Thanks a lot.'

'He's easily pleased,' Susan said quietly, when the surgeon and his registrar came out of the cubicle.

'Men,' Adam said dryly. 'We're simple creatures. Hello.'

'Hello.' Underneath his doctor's coat he was wearing jeans and a deep green polo-style shirt which turned his eyes even more intently emerald than usual. He looked dark and powerfully attractive, and despite her usual indifference to good-looking men she could feel herself reacting again to this one.

'Tony's good this morning,' she said unevenly. 'Obviously he still needs close supervision but things are improving slowly. The session last night went well, I think. We're having another one on Monday night if you're interested.'

For the first time she saw him look hesitant about something. 'Unless you think a surgical presence is essential, I might pass on that.'

'Your presence isn't essential.' Remembering his ill-concealed relief at her dismissal the evening before, she wasn't surprised he didn't want to attend another meeting. 'I don't imagine that sort of thing is your usual cup of tea.'

Hovering beside him, Christopher looked interested, but, as if registering his presence for the first time, the surgeon glanced at him, looked away and then looked back again.

'Churchill,' he said, with what Susan thought was unnecessary impatience. 'At nine.'

'Nine.' The younger man looked as if he wasn't about to move at first, but something in his consultant's expression must have changed his mind because he promptly swivelled and hurried off.

'Last night was…interesting,' Adam said, his gaze coming back to her.

'Confirmation that you made the right vocational choice?' she ventured.

'You've caught my emotion exactly.' He laughed. 'Remember I'm just a surgeon. I fix broken bones.'

'The principles are the same,' she argued gently, finding herself relaxing as she allowed herself to be captivated by the sheer perfection of his smile.

'The practices are profoundly different.'

'I know.' She shook her head in mocking bemusement. 'I'll make a confession. Setting bones is utterly beyond me. The practicalities of the process defeat me completely.'

Two creases appeared between his brows. 'You're not serious.'

It was only when they walked out into the foyer around the entrance lifts that she realised his hand at her back had gently swept her out of the ward.

'I *am* serious,' she insisted, too intent now on convincing him to mind when he urged her into the lift that opened in front of them. 'To get accepted into a psychiatric training programme I had to do six months as a casualty SHO. It only took a week for me, the consultant and every other doctor and nurse on staff to realise that it was never going to be safe to leave me to deal with a patient's bones. They banned me from the fracture clinic.'

He laughed again. 'I don't believe you.'

'It's true.' She started laughing herself. 'There's always been something about orthopaedics that I can't get my head around. Medicine, the rest of surgery, psychiatry—fine. But orthopaedics leaves me mystified. I've never been good at angles and visio-spatial stuff. Plus the theatre sessions leave me sick. The noise and all that…blood and bone flying around make me physically ill.'

'What did you do that first week in Casualty to make them ban you?'

'Nothing so bad,' she admitted. 'I didn't really do anything because I couldn't usually work out how to.' The memory of the hours she'd spent studying X-rays and trying to work out what was wrong with her patients and how to fix them was painfully embarrassing. 'I kept having to call the on-call orthopaedic staff down to Casualty to help me. I discovered that orthopaedic doctors can be very impatient, rude, ignorant and sarcastic human beings.'

'Especially when they're woken in the middle of the night to reduce a Colles' fracture,' he said dryly, referring to a common type of fracture of the lower end of the arm bones. 'Was that the sort of thing that upset them?'

'Exactly the sort of thing,' she confirmed. At the hospital where she'd done her casualty training, a Colles' fracture was an injury that tended to be dealt with by casualty officers who then referred the person for specialist orthopaedic examination the following day. Only in her case she'd never been able to stabilise the injury without immediate help.

They were up on one of the upper surgical floors now and she looked around, puzzled as his arm at her elbow guided her across the foyer. She'd assumed he was going to Churchill to meet his registrar but this wasn't the right floor. 'Adam…?'

'This way,' he said quietly, urging her forward.

'But aren't you meeting Christopher?'

'At nine,' he agreed.

Glancing at her wrist, she saw that that was only ten minutes away. Reassured, since nothing *too* worrying could happen in ten minutes, she looked around the pleasantly furnished foyer. 'What's Thatcher Ward?'

'Private plastics and neurosurgery. George, across there, is private orthopaedics. Haven't you ever worked on this side of the hospital?' There was a row of unmarked doors in the side-corridor and he unlocked one of them and opened it.

'Never. I've only done psychiatry here and none of it's over here. Adam—'

'I know, I know.' They were inside the office now and he drew her against him, closing the door with his back as he leaned against it. 'We're not suited,' he muttered. She felt as if he was playing with her, toying with her feelings, brushing his mouth against hers repeatedly but delicately, but he was so perfect and so male and intent on his task that she couldn't mind because just looking up at him made her ache.

'We have nothing in common.' His voice sounded as raw as her nerves. 'Forget that. Just shut up and feel.'

She'd known what he was going to do. Every taut, tingling little cell in her being had known it from the instant he'd drawn her out of the lift. But knowing it was going to happen and knowing that she shouldn't let it and that the sensible thing to do was to get as far away from him as she possibly could hadn't done anything to dull her senses or her craving for him and she went into him unreservedly.

'This is very, very bad,' she whispered, arching her neck as his mouth tracked along her throat. 'I told you I didn't want this.'

'You lied.' He already had her jacket off her shoulders and now his hands slid beneath her knitted top. 'You're a terrible liar.'

One hand went to each side of her and she was getting used to that, almost getting accustomed to the warm pressure of his hands against her midriff, but then abruptly, as if he couldn't stop himself, they slid higher. He captured the outer curves of her lace-covered breasts and squeezed them briefly together, but the intimacy was too shocking for her and she gasped and lifted her arms urgently to push his hands away.

'No,' she insisted. 'Adam, stop. Please—'

He didn't leave her, as she'd intended, but he cut off her plea with his mouth, soothing her with careful, gentle kisses as his hands withdrew.

Lost in the delightful tenderness of his kisses, she felt some of her shock recede.

'It's OK,' he whispered. 'I've stopped.' His hands were behind her now, spread across her back, reassuringly outside the protection of her top. 'It's OK. Look. I'm not touching you.'

But his mouth was. He teased her with it, biting softly at her lower lip until she let it open a little. Then he turned probing, stroking her lips and the tiny tip of flesh she felt brave enough to expose until she realised that she wanted more.

Waves of heat swept over her as she opened fully to the delicious, insistent pressure of his demanding kiss. His arms tightened around her and he lifted her harder against him so that she could feel the unmistakable pressure of his arousal against her stomach. She waited to feel shocked again but this time it didn't happen. Instead, the thought that she had the power to do that to him was intoxicating.

But slowly he untwined the hands she'd looped around

his neck and he pulled back from her. 'I have to go,' he said huskily.

As if he couldn't bear to go so soon, he kissed her again. Just briefly but hard. Then again. No hands this time, no embrace—just a kiss. Then once more.

'Churchill,' she said numbly.

'Wait for me?'

'I can't.' It wasn't just that it wasn't right although, despite her numbness, that was part of that. 'I've so much work to do. I'm on call this weekend. I've got a meeting with a patient's landlord, then…there're lots and lots of things that I have to do.'

His head came down and he touched her lips with his mouth again. 'Call me when you're free.'

'Adam,' she protested, bemused anew that she'd let him do this to her. 'We can't…you can't keep doing this. You know it isn't right.'

'I hear you.' But he was smiling. 'We're not suited. I'm too pushy and you're too intelligent for me,' he said teasingly. 'I know, Susan. I've heard it all before.' He opened the door and on his way out said, 'Call me.'

She didn't. Call him, that was. It wasn't that she was too busy. By seven in the evening there'd only been one admission and that had been a woman with chronic schizophrenia who'd only recently been discharged. Clare Laws was well known to all the medical and nursing staff and merely needed a temporary boost in her medication to control the hallucinations that were disturbing her. Susan's registrar instituted the changes without even needing to consult her.

The reason she was determined not to call Adam was that she was very certain that neither of them had anything to gain by any further contact and she felt that she, especially, had a lot to lose.

So in the early evening she still sat in her office trying to draft a letter to him, the crumpled paper collecting in her bin a symbol of how difficult it was to find the words.

It had taken a long time for the heat to drain away from her body that morning but when it eventually had she'd been left feeling weak and shaken. In retrospect the memory of the…wantonness of her behaviour appalled her. Brutally, she made no attempt to minimise her own contribution to the events, and the reality was awful. He hadn't forced anything upon her. The unpalatable truth was that not only had she not resisted his kisses, she'd actively encouraged him.

She'd given him every reason to assume that she was willing now for anything he suggested, but the cold reality was that she wasn't, she acknowledged wearily. Willing. And even if her traitorous body thought it was, her mind definitely wasn't.

She knew she owed him an explanation, some sort of apology, but since she'd bungled every attempt at giving him either one of those so far she didn't trust herself to confront him in person.

Only it wasn't proving any easier to do it in writing. She read her latest pathetically wordy letter dismally, then with a soft groan she balled it in her fist and dumped that one, too, into her bin. With years of psychiatric training and analysis behind her, one thing she should be good at was expressing her emotions and motivations but it seemed she wasn't.

The blare of her bleep provided a welcome distraction to her efforts, particularly when the only thing of any practical usefulness she'd achieved all day had been to convince Mrs Bibby's landlord that he should let her return to her flat.

She reached for the phone gladly and punched out the

number illuminated on her bleep. 'Susan Wheelan,' she said crisply. A woman's voice answered and identified herself as a casualty nurse. 'Someone bleeped me on that number.'

There was a brief muffled conversation and then a strong male voice demanded, 'Susan? Where are you?'

Her whole body stiffened. 'In my office,' she said thickly. 'At St Martin's. Adam—'

But she was too late. He'd hung up.

CHAPTER EIGHT

ADAM had never been to the psychiatric department at St Martin's. The hospital, close to London's northern outskirts, shared a huge, sprawling, tree-laden site with the university and, despite the years he'd been working there, he had no more than a vague idea of where Susan worked. But he found one faded signpost adjacent to the main surgical and medical block and from there he managed to muddle his way over there with only two wrong turns.

Parking his car in the section designated for staff cars, he depressed a button on his keyring to secure the vehicle. The four-storey building that squatted among three long, single-storey wards seemed the most likely site for the staff offices and he headed towards it.

But the automatic doors at the bottom of the block didn't open and there was no intercom or list of building occupants, forcing him to divert to the closest ward.

An elderly couple sat smoking just inside the glass doors surrounding the foyer, and he signalled to them, asking them to open the doors from the inside for him, but they stared back at him blankly.

The pair were fully dressed, instead of wearing pyjamas, so he assumed that they were visitors rather than patients and he tried knocking again. Finally the woman did stand up. She stubbed out her cigarette on the floor and shuffled towards him with ill-concealed reluctance. But instead of opening the doors she simply pressed her nose and lips against the glass until they became flattened and pale and the glass misted around her face.

Adam sighed. Looking more carefully, he saw a button above a small speaker in the wall and he reached across and pushed it.

'Adam Hargraves,' he said abruptly when a fuzzy, barely audible voice answered his bell. 'To see Dr Wheelan. Can I get though this way?'

Static came back at him but the door buzzed and he pushed it open, surprised to find himself needing to use considerable force because the deceptively frail-looking elderly woman on the other side now appeared determined to keep him out.

Murmuring apologies, Adam managed to gently dislodge her feet enough to squeeze himself in. But as he stopped to make sure that the door closed properly behind him it seemed she had a change of heart about his welcome because she forgot about trying to stop him getting in and instead embraced him.

Adam froze at the feel of wiry hands creeping around his front but the sensation of a head nestling into his back had him swivelling around fast and he carefully removed the woman from his person.

'How do you do?' he said, holding her hands away when they crept back towards him.

'I shall tell them you're here,' she said imperiously, although she made no move to leave.

'Thank you.' Adam managed a nod towards her companion who'd now finished his cigarette and had risen to watch them. 'Good evening.'

The man nodded back at him politely. 'Cats playing. Cats playing. Cats flaying. Bats praying.'

'Yes.' Adam wasn't sure what else he could contribute. 'Fine.' He'd spent four weeks as a medical student attached to a psychiatric ward, but that had been a long time

ago and he hadn't found the experience any less discon-
certing than he was finding this one. 'Thank you.'

Releasing the woman now that she seemed quite content
to simply stand and study him, he went to check the door
that led from the foyer into the taller block but it was
locked and clearly needed to be triggered by a security-
card device and he realised that he had little choice but to
go first onto the ward.

Nodding again as he passed the two acquaintances he'd
already made, he headed back the other way until he
reached another set of glass doors. This time he was
buzzed though without having to do anything. A door off
the corridor opened and a middle-aged bearded man in
jeans and a Led Zeppelin T-shirt poked his head out.

'Hi,' he chirped. 'Roy. You are…?'

'Adam Hargraves, looking for Susan Wheelan,' Adam
said heavily, guessing, from the home-rolled aroma of the
cigarette the other man held, that the hospital's strict no-
smoking ban had not yet spread as far as the psychiatric
department.

'Really?' The man called Roy looked interested. 'Susan.
Curious. Wow.'

'Is she here?' Adam asked, meaning on the ward as
opposed to in her office.

'Is it Saturday night?'

Adam frowned but Roy didn't seem to expect any reply
to the question because he simply unclipped a card from
one of the belt-loops on his jeans and passed it to him.

'It's a spare,' he told him. 'Leave it with her. Door at
the end there. Third floor. Have a groovy evening.'

'Thank you.'

In future, Adam decided, smiling then skirting widely
around the elderly couple to avoid the woman's out-

stretched arms, he'd meet Susan somewhere other than at her workplace.

He found her office, up three flights and through a secretary's area, by following the only lights on in the building. She was sitting behind a broad desk but her chair was tipped back and, clearly not having heard his approach, she had her eyes closed.

As always when he looked at her he felt his senses stir but for now there wasn't time to do anything about it. 'Susan...?'

She blinked her eyes wide open and he saw that despite his warning she was surprised by him appearing. 'Adam,' she said huskily. 'How did you get in without calling again?'

'Through Winchester Ward.'

'But...security.' She was frowning now. 'You're not supposed to be able to walk in like that. Who let you in?'

Adam wasn't interested in talking about that. He wasn't interested in talking about anything at all. Since leaving her that morning in his office it had been a struggle to think about anything but touching her and how soft and how willing she'd felt in his arms.

Fortunately his day had been busy. He'd spent most of the last two hours in Theatre, repairing the medial cartilage in the knee of a professional footballer who'd managed to partially rupture it during a play session with his toddler.

Years ago, when he'd been a registrar in training, he'd been taught to simply excise the damaged fragment. But since then the importance of the cartilage in stabilising the knee and protecting the working surfaces had been recognised. When the tear was along the small part of the meniscus that had a reasonable blood supply, he now repaired it.

The surgery had been delicate and demanding and it had

been a welcome distraction from his thoughts and his mounting frustration as Susan had still failed to call him.

'Susan—'

'Stay there,' she said sharply, making him stop although he'd only moved a couple of paces towards her. 'Don't come any closer. Adam, I don't want you to touch me. I've written to you.' She held up a sheet of paper and he saw that his name was at the top followed by a few close lines of writing, but from where he was standing he couldn't read it. 'Well, I've started to write it,' she amended. 'I'm writing to you to explain everything. It's going to take me a little while but in essence I don't think we should see each other again.'

Adam sighed, wondering why he hadn't predicted that. He'd assumed they'd made progress that morning, but apparently what he'd won he'd lost again. 'Don't write to me,' he said heavily. 'Tell me.' He held out one hand. 'Come to dinner and we'll talk.'

'Dinner?' She looked surprised, then her lovely eyes narrowed suspiciously behind her glasses. 'At your place?'

'Somewhere where there're lots of people.'

'I'm not dressed.'

'You look wonderful.' Inwardly he smiled, back, at least, on familiar territory here. Susan rarely reminded him of other woman, but in her concern about her clothes she was not so very different from some he'd known.

And his compliment had been an understatement. She looked enchanting and utterly desirable to him. Particularly when he thought about how soft her skin had felt beneath her top and jacket and especially when he allowed himself to consider how intoxicating the firm, warm press of her breasts against his palms had been.

She stood up, as if intending to come with him, although

she was still protesting. 'I don't even have any lipstick here—'

'Your lips are perfect.' He'd have liked to demonstrate how perfect he thought they were but her wary expression suggested she wouldn't appreciate it so he stayed where he was. 'Be daring,' he taunted gently. 'Live dangerously. We both have to eat and you shouldn't pass up one more opportunity to tell me how unsuitable I am.'

'Dinner in a public place,' she said warily, obviously not completely trusting him yet.

'With lots of other people around,' he supplied, smiling when after just one more doubtful look she collected her handbag.

Pleased with himself for managing to stop himself reaching out for her as she came gingerly past him, he confined himself instead to a gentle appreciation of her floral scent and a less gentle appreciation of the movement of her hips beneath the skirt of her suit as he followed her downstairs and out of the building.

It was dark outside and, although he couldn't see her expression clearly, he felt her uncertainty as she hesitated at the entrance to the car park. 'We're both on call,' she reminded him. 'I should take my car in case one of us is bleeped back. Where shall I meet you?'

Adam wasn't going to take a chance on her having second thoughts. 'We'll go in mine,' he said firmly, taking her elbow this time to guide her towards his car. 'If you're called back, I'll drive you. If I'm called back, I'll...get a lift and leave the car for you.' Christopher would be called if he was, and his registrar would have his car at the party. 'That's easiest,' he insisted, when she looked about to protest. 'Over here. By the way, who's Roy?'

'Roy?' Apparently distracted enough by the question to forget her doubts, she came along with him unresistingly.

'On Winchester Ward. Hippie-type person.' He bleeped open his car and opened the passenger door for her. 'Five-eight, long grey beard, bad nicotine habit.'

'Bad nicotine…?' Buckling her seat belt, she blinked up at him enchantingly. 'He was smoking?'

'Is he nurse or patient?' After shutting his door, he went around to the driver's side, climbed in and started the engine. 'If he's a patient then you've got a security problem because he was carrying a spare pass.'

'He's the psych unit's charge nurse,' she said absently, as if the fact was unsurprising. 'Roy was *smoking*?'

Checking his mirrors, Adam reversed out of the park. 'I didn't see anyone on that ward who wasn't.'

'But he's given up. He hasn't smoked in more than a year. He had hypnosis. And therapy. Duncan took him for six sessions of aversion therapy to reinforce the hypnosis.'

'Then I understand why he didn't tell anyone he'd started again,' Adam murmured. The verve with which the older psychiatrist had delivered his lecture on torture methods still concerned him a little. And his recall of med-school psychology told him that aversion therapy involved pairing unwanted behaviour with a punishment. 'Do you think Duncan used the spinning-chair therapy?'

'Of course not.' She sounded irritated. 'Duncan's a very gentle person. And, besides, his special interest isn't classic aversion therapy as you probably think of it. He uses a psychological technique called covert sensitisation. It involves just thinking about the punishment, rather than having it carried out. In Roy's case Duncan taught him to associate the first puff of a cigarette with being on a ferry crossing the Channel in a storm. Since Roy's prone to terrible seasickness, it seemed likely to work.'

Concentrating on the road and the heavy Saturday night traffic rather than on what she was saying, Adam thanked his good fortune again for his success in a profession that didn't require any discussion of words like 'covert' and 'sensitisation' along with the interplay of concepts like aversion and therapy.

He could grasp the more practical aspects of psychiatry—the lists of requirements for the diagnosis of specific medical conditions such as schizophrenia and depression and their respective pharmacological treatments—but the more ethereal conditions, the neuroses and their intangible psychological therapies, left his head buzzing.

Like most surgeons, he suspected, he respected the sort of work Susan did. But he didn't pretend to understand it.

'So, you see, Duncan's not some sort of depraved sadist,' she was saying now, 'but a highly skilled, gifted psychiatrist. I admire him tremendously.'

'He certainly seems to have a number of special interests,' Adam commented. 'Do you have any?'

'Broadly speaking, my main interest is in the assessment of suicide risk,' she told him. 'At present I'm setting up a study which is going to be looking into the prevalence of psychiatric illness among parasuicide presentations at St Martin's Casualty Department. Our main problem is going to be that assessing whether a patient is psychiatrically ill or not isn't always easy. Depression and the psychotic illnesses are fairly straightforward but once you get into some of the more borderline personality disorders then things become very complicated. Oh—' After sounding enthusiastic, she stopped, then added apologetically, 'Parasuicide means attempted suicide. Sorry. I'm probably getting too technical.'

Amused, he sent her a sideways look. 'I'm keeping up,' he said evenly. 'Just. Carry on. I'm interested.'

'I'm sure you're just being polite,' she said quietly.

'Indulge me.' He braked for the red light ahead of him,

sparing her another look once they'd stopped. 'You could put it in little words if you're worried I won't understand you.'

'You think I'm patronising you.'

'You are.' He laughed. 'But I don't mind,' he said easily. 'Patronise away.'

'I do admire what you do,' Susan said gently. 'But, Adam, you must be aware that orthopaedic surgery doesn't exactly attract the intellectual cream of graduating doctors.'

'Does it not?' Adam's mouth quirked as he accelerated away from the lights. 'And all these years I've assumed that all the dullards went into gynae.'

'Gynaecology?' She sounded surprised. 'I've never heard that before.'

'Gynaecologists only have to learn variations on two operations. If anything goes wrong with those they call in the experts to repair the damage. It might be more complicated than that but that's how the job looks to every other surgeon.'

Barbara and Lawrence lived in the next street on the left and he signalled and turned and pulled up behind the parked cars which had occupied all spaces up to about four houses away.

'Adam…?'

'Relax,' he murmured, coming around to open her door. 'Annabel's here.'

'Annabel?' He'd thought the mention of her sister's presence would reassure her but instead she looked appalled. 'What?'

'It's Barbara and Lawrence's,' he said smoothly. 'So you already know five people. Six if you count Chris McInnes, my registrar. Barbara's doing dinner.'

'You've brought me to a…party?'

'Dinner,' he repeated, leading her forward gently when she seemed about to resist him.

'But I don't go to parties.'

'Then it's time you started.' Unable to stop himself, he bent forward and touched her startled, deliciously open lips with his mouth. 'You're doing dangerous things to my blood pressure, looking at me like that,' he murmured. 'Close your mouth, Susan, sweetheart. Or I'll have to take you back to the car and attempt something I haven't tried in such a confined space in twenty years.'

Obviously finding that suggestion far more alarming than any horrors Barbara's dinner might supply, the psychiatrist closed her mouth sharply and marched ahead of him to the door of his sister's home.

Despite the frost already crisping the grass between the flagstones that made up the path from the gate, the front door into the main living area was open. Light and heat from the huge fire Lawrence was guarding and noise from the twenty or so people gathered in the room spilled out to welcome them as they approached.

As they reached the door, Adam deliberately slid his arm around Susan.

'Adam! Adam, finally.' Adam suspected that Lawrence's flushed and exuberant greeting stemmed more from the generous measure of spirits in the glass he clutched than from the heat of the fire.

'We thought you must have been stuck at work,' Lawrence added, almost bubbling. 'Susan, you look gorgeous.' He stepped forward as if to embrace her, but a warning look from Adam sent him backing off again with appropriate haste. 'Everybody, this is Susan. You all know Barbara's brother, Adam.'

There was a round of general greetings and nods of acknowledgement, and Adam exchanged a few words with a couple of Lawrence's and Barbara's neighbours as they moved through into the room.

When he turned back to Susan, Lawrence was trying to tempt her to drink. 'How about a Long Island iced tea?' he was asking. 'Didn't you like that one I gave you on Tuesday night?'

'I'd prefer something soft,' Susan answered firmly. 'Entirely soft. Thank you.'

'Straight cola,' Adam ordered, suspecting that Lawrence, who considered alcohol one of life's greatest gifts, would be unlikely to be swayed by Susan's insistence.

'Adam, where have you been...? Susan!' Barbara emerged from the kitchen and Adam registered the singularly murderous look she sent him when she saw his companion. 'What a— Hello.'

Prising her way between them with an agility he could only admire, Barbara bumped him out of the way and drew the psychiatrist in the other direction. 'It's so lovely to see you again,' she said, mouthing something rude in his direction before directing a very pointed look at her husband.

'Have you met Christopher, Adam's registrar?' he could hear her asking Susan as the two women moved away. 'He's *so* nice. Not at all like Adam.' Again he got a glare. 'He's just over here, eating all my peanuts,' Barbara continued. 'Come and talk to him.'

'I think that was my cue to introduce you to your partner for the evening,' Lawrence chirped, close to his ear. 'Monica happens to be in the next room. This way. Low trick, Adam.'

'It wasn't a trick.' Ignoring Lawrence's stuttered protests, Adam went after Susan.

He stopped Barbara a few words into what sounded as if it was going to be an elaborate introduction. 'They've met,' he interrupted, sending Christopher a hard look when he saw the younger man's delighted smile at being paired with Susan, however temporarily. 'Introduce Christopher to your special guest, Babs. I'll look after Susan.'

Not giving any of them a chance to protest, he drew the psychiatrist away. 'Ignore Barbara,' he murmured, steering her in the direction of the kitchen where he thought there'd be a better chance of getting her alone. 'She thinks she's protecting you but Christopher's far more dangerous than me.'

'I doubt it.' But she smiled a little. 'Why am I here?'

'I wanted you to be.'

'But why?'

'Partly to protect me,' he murmured, drawing her forward into the darkened alcove of Barbara's pantry.

'From your sister?'

He explained briefly about the teacher who'd answered Barbara's advertisement. 'Babs has been pestering me all week.'

'But the girl sounds perfect,' she protested.

'For Christopher,' he agreed, focusing on the lusciously full curve of her lower lip. 'But if I'd come alone there would have been no deflecting her.'

The lip puckered. 'Adam, but now everyone thinks *we're* together.'

'Mmm.' He lowered his head. 'Terrible, isn't it?' They were in their own private space but there were people all around him and he could hear Lawrence pontificating from the living room and he couldn't kiss her because if he touched her mouth he didn't think he'd be able to stop.

'I've been thinking about you all day,' he muttered. He pulled her deeper into the darkness until his back came up hard against Barbara's preserve-laden shelves. 'Imagining you. Wanting to hold you. Touch you. Kiss you. And now…now here I can't do a thing about it. You're driving me slowly insane.'

'I'm driving myself insane.' It was a soft, husky imprecation and it seemed to come reluctantly from her, but it made his head spin. 'I don't know what to do.'

'I have a suggestion.'

'I expect you do.' Her breathlessness and the tentative, delicious touch of her fingers against his chest made him shudder. 'I know this can't go on,' she added. 'I know I should be being sensible, but when I'm with you—when I'm actually close to you, like this—I can't think straight.'

'I don't want you to think straight.' He hadn't thought straight since meeting her.

He knew that, like that morning, she'd pull away if he went near her breasts again but he'd got his hands up to her midriff now, so close to them that he knew if he inched just a fraction higher he'd feel her beginning to swell above his fingers and his hands trembled with the effort of staying still.

Shapes—two, then two more—flashed past the pantry entrance and he froze, reminded abruptly of where they were. Despite wanting to make it clear to Barbara that her matchmaking efforts were doomed, he didn't want Susan embarrassed by being caught in any compromising position with him, and he was angry with himself for not taking more care.

'I promise we'll just eat and run,' he said tightly. 'Think you can you manage that?'

Even in the dimness of the pantry he could see that her flushed face wore a confused expression but her nod in response to his question was reassuringly swift. 'And then you'll take me back to the hospital.'

He smoothed her hair. 'And then I'll take you away from here,' he compromised.

He could tell from the way she stiffened and her sharp intake of breath that she'd understood, but he didn't let her argue. Warm food smells were drifting from the kitchen and now that his body had acknowledged that fulfilment of his most pressing desire was impossible immediately he found himself hungry. 'Dinner,' he declared, going forward to check that the passage was clear before he drew her out. 'Let's eat.'

CHAPTER NINE

ANNABEL and Mike, late as usual, arrived just as Susan finished dishing herself a selection of curries from the massive buffet Adam's sister had prepared—and about two minutes after she'd finally reassured herself that they could not possibly be coming.

Observing the usual dramatic embraces and kisses which invariably accompanied Annabel's arrival anywhere, Susan wondered how it was that her sister managed to create such a fuss when she couldn't possibly know any more people here than Susan did.

Keeping her head lowered, she made a determined effort to find a seat somewhere isolated but Annabel, from the midst of the crowd, squealed at her.

'Susie,' she cried. 'And…Adam.' Susan saw her making purposefully for the surgeon. 'What a delicious surprise. I didn't know you were coming. Certainly not together.' A narrowed glare from Annabel before she launched herself at Adam told Susan that she should prepare to be harangued about that particular fact later. 'Kiss me, Adam, you gorgeous man. It feels like months since I've seen you.'

'It's been four days,' Susan pointed out, enjoying Adam's startled efforts to extricate himself from her sister's determined embrace, 'the first of which you spent in a hung-over daze.'

'Thank you,' Annabel said, pursing her lips into a mock kiss as Adam finally succeeded in putting her away from him without succumbing to the lip-to-lip contact she'd

150

clearly wanted. 'Thank you very much. So...?' She brushed her palms together briskly. 'Done the deed yet?'

Susan winced, not only at her sister's crassness, but also at the thickness of the cloud of perfume and alcohol that enveloped her when she tried to kiss her cheek. 'Go away,' she ordered Annabel. 'Food's that way. I have a feeling you need it.'

'Sorry.' Mike mouthed the word and made violent drinking gestures as he bundled his wife away. 'Vodka martinis,' he murmured to her and Adam as they passed. 'All afternoon.'

'I know it looks bad but she doesn't actually drink that much.' For reasons which at that moment were beyond her, Susan found herself defending Annabel to Adam as they found seats in the living room. 'The problem is that it only takes a couple to turn her silly.'

'Have you any other brothers or sisters?'

She shook her head. 'Like you mentioned once before about your own parents, our parents had us very late. My mother was forty when I was born so by the time Annabel came along she couldn't have had any more even if she'd wanted to.'

'Annabel's younger than you?'

She met his sharp comment with a nod, used to that sort of surprised reaction. Annabel might not look older, but her manner always gave that impression. 'Not that she's ever acted younger,' she conceded. 'Even when we were children she was always the one who took charge. I used to think having her around was like having an extra mother, only Mum wasn't at all nosy or interfering like Annabel.'

'Do your parents live in London?'

'They used to live in Kent. We grew up in Tunbridge Wells. Mum died suddenly the year I started my first registrar job and Dad died two years ago.' Susan swallowed firmly. She'd come to terms with the deaths of her parents and her memories were all good ones, but she missed them terribly and thinking about that loss still often saddened her.

'There's just Annabel and me now.' She looked down at the rice on her fork. 'And Mike. And Emma, of course, my niece.'

Neither of them said much more while they finished their food and then one of the neighbours came across, obviously keen to talk to Adam, so Susan excused herself and went to see if there was anything she could do to help in the kitchen.

But Barbara already had plenty of helpers and she shooed her out. Susan ended up in conversation with a couple of Barbara's golfing friends, after which she drifted around, making small talk with some of the other guests, aware from time to time that Adam was watching her as she circulated, doing her best to avoid Annabel.

It was a strange feeling, knowing that he was there and that they were together. She wasn't used to being part of a couple and although she knew it wasn't real she found herself secretly enjoying it.

Chris seemed to be getting on very well with the woman Barbara had intended for Adam. The two had sat laughing and chatting together for most of the evening so far, and Christopher's eyes were shining.

Young love, she thought whimsically, contemplating how much less complicated her own life would have been if she'd met someone ten years earlier, who'd affected her the way Adam did now.

Then sex would have been a far simpler thing. Ten years ago she'd not have worried about devoting time to an affair that had no future. But now that did worry her. It worried her that becoming involved with Adam might mean she missed meeting some other man who might otherwise have been a potential father for her children.

Adam was talking to Mike, and she studied the surgeon pensively.

Ten years ago she also wouldn't have been concerned about giving up something which would now be a very special gift for a husband for the sake of satisfying a physical urge she wished she didn't possess.

'Just do it.' Annabel lurched against her, bumping her shoulder as she waved a wobbly hand in Adam's direction, but her comment told Susan that unfortunately her mental faculties weren't as impaired as her physical ones. 'You're mad if you don't, Susie. He's divine. What if you never meet anyone else?'

'What if I do meet someone else but I don't notice him because I'm too preoccupied with Adam?' she said forlornly. 'I'm not young any more, Annie.'

'Stop examining every little thing.' Annabel flapped her hands dismissively. 'I hate the way you do that. Why can't you just be normal?'

Susan sighed. 'So what's normal? Just doing what feels good and hang the consequences?'

'At least you admit it feels good.' Annabel pinched her arm and chuckled. 'That's a start, Susie. You've never done that before.'

'Feeling good doesn't mean it feels right.'

'Take some words of advice from a woman with a lot of experience,' Annabel said sagely, wavering slightly from side to side. 'If it doesn't feel right with Adam, it's not going to feel right with any man. You're wasting your time waiting for someone else.'

'I'm not talking physical right, I'm talking emotional right,' Susan said wearily. 'There is a difference.'

'Well, he's doing something right,' Annabel declared. 'He's got you out to a party on a Saturday night. The only time that's happened before was my wedding.'

'Weekends are a very productive time for me.'

'Yes, yes. Heard it all before.' Her sister pulled a face. 'No interruptions. No phone calls. No clinics. Nothing that could possibly bring any interest into your…ghastly, horrible office.'

'No Rachel,' Susan said automatically. She was very fond of her secretary but it wasn't always easy to stop her talking.

Annabel's face went red. 'Well, no fun either, Susan. Just remember that this is your *life*,' she hissed. 'Not a dress rehearsal.'

Susan rolled her eyes. She'd been thinking that she hadn't heard that for a while. Annabel had been trotting out the little motto for years, initially to justify her own excesses but in recent years to condemn what she saw as Susan's lack of them.

'Come and I'll get you some coffee,' she said gently, leading her sister back towards the table where Barbara and her helpers were busily laying out pretty little jelly triangles and diamond-shaped custards. 'Annie, perhaps it's time you started cutting back on the hard spirits.'

From the kitchen she heard, a little later, the high-pitched tone of someone's bleep, but since she knew that these days all sorts of people carried the devices she barely gave it a thought until Adam came in briskly, obviously looking for her.

'Keys,' he said, passing her two attached to what looked like a tiny padded calculator. 'Triple four, four will release the locks. Sorry. There's been a coach accident on the M1. Chris and I are both going to be needed. Will you be all right?'

'Fine,' she said automatically, puzzled that he thought he had to ask.

He didn't kiss her but he ruffled her hair before he turned away. 'This'll probably take all night. I'll call you tomorrow.'

Susan wasn't sure what to do with his car. Almost as soon as he'd left she realised she should have told him to take it himself because she could have asked for a lift with Annabel and Mike. She suggested to Barbara that she should leave the car at the house for Adam to collect when he was finished at the hospital, but his sister refused to take the responsibility.

'If Lawrence sees it out there he'll have it halfway to Scotland before morning,' she said crisply. 'He's been slavering over the blasted thing for months. I don't even know why Adam bought it in the first place—spending that much money on a car's a complete waste of money as far as I can see. Don't take it home, for heaven's sake. He'll only take that as an invitation to visit you. Leave it at the hospital somewhere. It'll be safer there than here.'

Knowing that the car was expensive, Susan felt nervous. As she prepared to leave a short while later she had another attempt at persuading Barbara to let her leave it there but the other woman still refused.

The keypad worked first time—triple four, four was the emergency code for the St Martin's bleep system so she didn't have any trouble remembering it—but once inside the car and buckled up she hesitated. Normally a confident driver, she contemplated the controls doubtfully.

Her own car was an eleven-year-old compact and not zippy at all. She hadn't even noticed when Adam had driven her here but now that she did she realised that this one looked new and exceedingly zippy.

Experimentally, she drove around Barbara's quiet suburban block so that by the time she had to tackle a main road she had a feel for the light pressure she needed to apply to the accelerator to keep the monster under control on the icy roads. Surprisingly, though, it wasn't difficult to drive. The steering was lighter than on her own car and the vehicle's immediate responsiveness to her commands, though it took a little getting used to, boosted her confidence.

Barbara's advice about not taking the car to her flat was sound, she decided, turning into the main hospital area at St Martin's. She definitely didn't want to encourage a visit from Adam. She left the car in the staff area behind the surgical block and walked from there to the psychiatric department, belting her coat tightly over her jacket to keep out the clear evening's wintry chill.

It was almost ten. Because she wanted to leave a message with the switchboard operator to tell Adam where to find his car, she went towards the nearest ward to use an internal telephone. 'All quiet,' Roy drawled, coming out of Winchester on his way off duty as she was opening her bag to retrieve her security card. 'So where've you been tonight, mysterious lady?' He held the door open for her. 'Heavy date with the Adam man?'

Susan sighed, contemplating her secretary's reaction to such a piece of information as she walked inside. 'How about you say nothing to Rachel about Adam Hargraves and I say nothing to Duncan about you smoking again?'

'Sweet.' With an easy grin, the nurse pulled the motorcycle helmet he'd been carrying down over his face. 'I'm an easygoing being but that aversion stuff he's into was too heavy. I was feeling seasick if I saw someone smoking fifty yards away. It took weeks of heavy smoking to wean that therapy out of my system. Another session with Duncan would break me. Good sleeping.'

'You, too.' She waved him off as she went on towards the ward. As he'd declared, Winchester was quiet, and she did a brief round of the nurses on the other two wards to check that there were no potential problems before she went home.

Bells woke her. It took her a little time to realise that it was morning and light and that the insistent noise was coming from inside her flat rather than from the chapel at St Martin's. Rolling over and struggling out of bed, she fumbled for her glasses, sliding them on as she stumbled to the intercom. 'Yes?'

'It's Adam.'

Adam. She shook her head, still muzzy after being woken from what must have been a deep sleep. 'Sorry, I forgot about leaving the keys,' she said finally. 'Just a minute. I'll get them.'

She released the building's outside door so that he could wait out of the cold in the centrally heated foyer, but by the time she'd pulled on a coat and collected his car keys from her bag there was knocking at her door.

'Here.' Opening the door, she pushed the keys out to him. 'I'm sorry. I should have left them at the hospital for you.'

'I had spares.' He shoved the keys into the side pocket of his jeans. He was, she realised, wearing the same clothes he'd been wearing the night before. Ignoring the way she was shielding herself behind the door, he firmly eased it open until the gap was wide enough for him to come in. Once inside, he eyed the coat she was wearing speculatively. 'Going somewhere?'

'I—I was coming down to meet you,' she stammered, hastily fastening the rest of the garment's buttons. 'Adam...'

But he strolled away from her, inspecting her tidy little

flat with apparent interest. 'I wouldn't have guessed you
were the sort to lie around in bed all morning.'

'I'm not,' she protested, bemused by the ease with
which he seemed prepared to make himself welcome. She
normally woke and rose promptly at six-thirty, but—probably because of the restless night she'd had—her body's
internal alarm hadn't functioned that morning. 'And it's
only eight-thirty.'

'I'm not complaining.' He was looking around her
kitchen now and his grin made her heart skip. 'About you
being in bed. Ready to go back?'

'No!' She brushed her hair back from her face with a
shaky hand then pushed her glasses higher on her nose.
'How did you know where I live?' She wasn't listed and
the hospital was supposed to keep personal information
confidential.

'Annabel told me.'

'Last night?'

'The day after we first met.' He regarded her steadily.
'She called me the next morning.'

'I just bet she did.' Susan gritted her teeth. The thought
of what that conversation might have been about appalled
her. 'Were the roses her idea?'

'All mine.' Shaking his head gently, he came across to
her, and close up she saw that despite his alertness he
looked tired. The stubbled roughness of his face told her
he'd not yet shaved and the usually vivid whites of his
eyes were crisscrossed with red.

'Susan, I didn't come for the keys.'

'I'll make you breakfast.' Ducking her head to avoid the
hand he lifted to her face, she went around him. 'You've
obviously been working all night. You must be hungry. I
haven't had a chance to listen to the news. Was it a serious
accident?'

'Two dead. Thirty injured. Ten seriously.'

She felt sick. 'Any children?'

'St Martin's took half the casualties and they were all adults.'

'You must still be very busy.' She'd taken a carton of eggs out of the fridge but now she hesitated. 'Do you have time for this?'

'Things are under control. I'm due back in Theatre at twelve unless I'm called earlier.'

'You're only five minutes away here,' she said, promptly feeling silly because, of course, after coming from the hospital just now he had to know that. 'Scrambled or boiled?'

'Whatever. You're still wearing your coat.'

'Yes.' Deliberately turning away from him, she broke two eggs into a bowl, added milk, started to whisk them together, thought about it, then stopped and added another egg.

'So do you usually wear your coat indoors?'

'Not usually.' She adjusted the flame beneath the sauce-pan and added a piece of butter. 'Two slices of toast enough?'

'Perfect. Are you cold? Shall I adjust the heating?'

'The heating's fine.' With the bread in the toaster, she poured the egg mixture into the pan and pulled a wooden spoon out of one of the drawers beside the cooker. 'I liked your car. It's much easier to drive than it looks.'

'Susan, whatever you're wearing underneath there can't possibly be any scantier than what you're making me imagine it is,' he growled. 'Believe me, keeping the coat on isn't helping.'

It was helping her. Avoiding his gaze, she took the eggs off the heat and put the lid on the pan to let them set. She busied herself, buttering his toast. 'Eat,' she said finally, dishing the eggs and pushing them towards him—leaving her free to escape. 'Salt and pepper are in the grinder there. Give the coffee a minute before you plunge it.'

She took a two-minute shower then dressed quickly, ran a stick of pink gloss across her mouth and roughly brushed out her hair. When she re-emerged he'd finished his breakfast and the coffee level in the plunger suggested he was onto his second mug.

'Thanks,' Adam said calmly. 'For the food. It was good.' He surveyed her nervous figure dispassionately. 'Do you ever wear anything but suits?'

Susan blinked, confused by the unexpectedness of the question. 'Like what?'

'Like casual clothes. Like jeans. Or T-shirts. Like anything that doesn't have a jacket.'

'I... Sometimes,' she said huskily, fingering one of the buttons of the jacket he seemed to find so unappealing. 'I have some jeans.'

'When's the last time you wore them?'

'Last year on holiday.' She felt herself frown in response to his exasperated look. 'It's different for you. You probably spend half the day in theatre gear. I have a professional image to maintain—'

'It's Sunday.'

'I go into work on Sundays.'

'You *have* to go in, or you go in to do paperwork?'

'Paperwork and research,' she admitted. 'Aside from emergencies, there's no clinical work for me on a Sunday. But my other work's important. As soon as I get rid of you that's where I'm going.'

'As soon as you get rid of me.' Green eyes narrowed. 'You know that's not going to happen in a hurry.'

'You can't stay.'

'That doesn't mean I'm planning to rush away.' In one

fluid movement he drained his coffee then swung around and came towards her.

She backed, but not quickly enough because—as if he had every right to do whatever he wanted—he caught her cheeks between his palms and held her face still and kissed her mouth.

'Mmm. Strawberry.' He licked her gloss away then tasted her again. 'Where's the shower?'

'Through the bedroom,' she said numbly. 'There're some disposable razors in the bottom drawer if you want to shave. Spare towels under the basin.'

'I'll use yours,' he said over his shoulder, leaving her. 'No sense in creating more work for you.'

'Do all men do things like this?' she demanded, not moving.

'Like what?'

'Like walking into a woman's home uninvited and then taking over.'

'Why go grey, waiting for an invitation that may never come?'

'Politeness,' she called. 'Courtesy. Good manners.'

Before the sound of water running into the basin drowned out any other noise she heard him laugh.

Biting at her lower lip, not sure exactly what she should do next, Susan surveyed the dishes left from her breakfast preparation. The washing-up would keep her busy at least. She began stacking plates, but then the shower started and she realised that if she used the hot water it would turn the shower frigid. The thought of drenching him in icy water was temporarily tempting, but, knowing what a demanding night he'd had, she couldn't bring herself to do it.

Instead, she poured the last of the coffee into another mug, sat at the breakfast bar and leafed through the previous day's *Guardian*, wondering who she thought she was trying to kid by pretending to be serene and unruffled while inwardly she trembled.

However much she told herself she was indifferent to the hiss of the shower's water supply, she still jumped about six inches in the air when it shut off. Gripping the edges of the newspaper very firmly, she stayed rigidly still, staring at the text although she hadn't read a word.

She heard the sound of her shower's glass door sliding open, heard him moving about and then coming through the bedroom. Although she felt him behind her she still jumped when he tucked her hair away from her right ear.

'I missed you,' he murmured, close to her. 'I had to wash my own back.'

She took a deep breath, refusing to look at him. 'Adam, I really think—'

'I don't,' he said softly, 'want you to think.'

She was on a swivel chair and he turned it around, forcing her to look at him. Relief that he wore a towel warred with panic at the involuntary way her hand lifted to press its palm to his naked chest.

She snatched it away immediately, but her shock at the gesture distracted her sufficiently that she barely protested when, with an approving murmur, he slid one arm beneath her knees and the other around her back and without any apparent effort lifted her right out of her seat.

'I'm not going to do anything,' he murmured, holding her fast when she began to struggle as they neared her bedroom. 'I'm too tired to do you justice and there's not enough time. I just want to rest and hold you for a little while.'

Susan didn't know what to do. It felt too unreal. She felt as if she were in a dream and the strangeness of the feeling rendered her sluggish and hesitant. With her brain she knew that he needed to rest and on a human level she wanted to give him comfort and he'd made the fact that he was holding her sound innocent.

Only there was nothing innocent about the determined fingers that unbuttoned her jacket as soon as he released her onto her feet beside her bed.

She lifted her hands to his wrists to stop him but her strength was puny compared with his and he didn't take any notice.

'It'll crease,' he murmured, sliding the fabric off her shoulders.

'You're undressing me,' she protested, when he brought her forward against him and unfastened the zip at the back of her skirt.

'Just your clothes,' he said, and she nodded at that, reassured until she realised what he'd said.

But by then he had her blouse over her head and she was down to her slip. It was full length and modestly cut, and she was covered enough not to feel too self-conscious, but it still felt strange. 'Adam—'

'Just these,' he promised, his thumbs sliding her tights free from her hips. 'You'll be more comfortable. Don't worry so.' He crouched and freed the nylon one foot at a time, then stood up again. A gentle thumb probed her softly bitten lower lip. 'That's all. See? You can leave everything else.'

'Don't take off your towel,' she warned.

'I'm not taking it off.'

'I don't trust you.'

'That's probably wise.' He answered her alarmed look with a wry smile. 'But now I just need to rest,' he said softly. 'I promise. Lie down. Sleep.'

Bemused by the knowledge of her own complicity, she

found herself sliding beneath the ruffled bedclothes. 'But I'm not even tired.'

'Then just lie beside me and think.' He came in behind her. One warm hand slid around her waist and he tugged her back against him. He lifted one leg over hers, entwining it between hers so that she could feel him like a warm wrapping around her from her shoulders to her ankles. 'Mmm, that feels good,' he said heavily. 'I like that.' His hand closed around her midriff below her left breast. 'Wake me in a couple of hours.'

His body relaxed and, judging from the slow steadiness of his breathing, he fell asleep almost immediately. But Susan lay there for what seemed like hours, rigid, too frightened to move in case it woke him, listening to her own frantically beating pulse as it was transmitted back to her through her pillow.

From time to time she lifted her head a little to check the clock on her bedside table, but even when she was sure that his two hours absolutely had to be up she saw that it was still ten minutes short of one hour.

She'd never shared a bed before. Until meeting him, she'd never even been held this close to any man before. She could no more have slept than...given birth to a chicken.

Not that it felt so terribly awful, she conceded finally a little way into the second hour. There was something...seductive in being held like this. With Adam asleep, the masculine pressure of his body against hers felt no less startling or powerful than usual but marginally less alarming. She felt...small. Protected. And...aroused, she admitted finally, unable to deny her body's slow, languid softening.

At eleven-fifteen she moved one leg. 'Adam?' she whispered. Dislodging his arm, she wriggled around and half sat up. 'Adam? Wake up.'

He opened his eyes slowly but the green sharpness of his regard told her that he was almost immediately alert. 'Was I bleeped?'

'You told me to wake you in two hours.'

'OK. Thanks.' He lifted his thigh, freeing hers, then swung his legs over the edge of her bed. He refastened the towel, which must have come undone while they were sleeping, in smooth, easy movements. 'Did you sleep?'

Aware that his eyes had dropped to the swell of her breasts, visible beneath the fabric of her slip, she slid down in the bed, covering herself with the duvet again. 'I was wide awake.'

'Shame.' The regard with which he'd observed her manoeuvre intensified. 'If you want, I know a nice way to make you feel sleepy again.'

'No, thank you.' The flush she'd felt starting at her breasts now crept up to cover her face and scalp. 'That won't be necessary.'

'Much as you appreciate the offer,' he said softly, looking amused.

Fortunately, since her tongue felt as if it had become too thick for her to manage speech, it seemed she wasn't expected to respond to that because he hauled himself off the bed and padded into her bathroom without giving her another look.

She saw the towel drop as he stepped towards the shower and averted her eyes sharply. She scrambled off the bed and went to pull on her suit, then hesitated as she remembered his earlier comments about her clothes. She looked at the jacket, trying to see it as other people might, then, with a murmured imprecation, she put it back onto its hanger. Cross with herself for feeling that she had any need to prove herself, she still found her legs taking her across to the drawers on the other side of the room.

'Susan, I'm going to be tied up the rest of the day—' Dressed now, he'd come to the sitting room, looking for her, but he stopped, and she felt herself blushing anew at his obvious surprise. 'Nice,' he said calmly. 'Very nice. You look lovely.'

'They're just jeans.' She looked down at herself, tugging a little uneasily at the white designer T-shirt Annabel had bought her for her birthday. She hadn't worn it before. Out of its packet it had looked alarmingly small but it had seemed to fit when she'd pulled it on. The only mirror in the flat larger than a compact was in the bathroom where he'd been showering so she hadn't been able to check herself yet. 'I thought…well, this might be a size too small.'

'You look perfect.'

'Obviously I'll wear a jumper as well in this weather,' she said, stiffening as he crossed the room.

'I like you as you are.' Catching her waist, he slid his arms around her and across her back and kissed her mouth. 'You look very young. Touchable. Eminently kissable.'

'Which doesn't mean I am,' she protested, twisting away from his hold and from the dangerously determined glint in his eyes. She retreated to the kitchen again, behind the bar where he'd breakfasted.

There was silence for a few tense moments and then he said, 'Which means what, Susan?' He sounded weary again and she was furious with herself for actually feeling guilty about reversing the benefits of his sleep.

'Are you saying that you're going to hold me off for ever?' he demanded quietly. 'That you're still determined to stay physically chaste while you wait in solitude for the perfect man? That until you find the man who fits every criterion on some ludicrous list you've dreamed up no one else is going to be allowed to come close?'

'It's my life,' she said hollowly, his words churning around in her head. 'I can live it the way I choose.'

'You're living in a fantasy world.'

'I don't expect you to understand.'

'You're right,' he said heavily. 'I don't.

She crossed her arms defensively across her chest. 'Adam, you haven't even tried to understand me. Almost all my life I've had Annabel pushing me around, trying to manipulate me—trying to get me to behave the way she thinks I should behave. I don't need someone else doing the same thing.'

She was holding herself so tensely that her arms were starting to ache, and she watched his face slowly close as what she was saying got through to him.

Finally, when his expression was a mask, he said, 'It's OK, Susan. I get the message. I'm sorry if I've…'

But the words drifted off into silence and then he checked his watch as if the time was important to him. 'I won't bother you any more. Thanks for the food and…the rest.'

'That's all right.' Mouthing the platitude automatically, she followed him to the door. 'I hope it's not so busy that you can't get some sleep tonight.'

'Let me know if there's anything you need for Tony.'

'I will. Thank you.'

He didn't say goodbye and neither did she because the word was everywhere in the air around them. She stayed in the hall until the door slammed downstairs. Her throat felt dry and raw.

She'd wanted him to go away and leave her alone. He'd only done what she'd wanted. So why did it suddenly feel as if a big page had turned over in her life and there was no way she'd ever be able to turn it back?

CHAPTER TEN

THREE weeks later Adam was able to discharge the first of the trauma patients who'd been seriously injured in the M1 coach accident. A fit sixty-two-year-old who'd suffered facial fractures and a broken tibia and fibula among other injuries, Mrs Perry was managing now to get around in a weight-bearing plaster. Her husband had received only minor injuries in the crash and he'd been discharged much earlier. He was well enough to look after his wife so Adam was happy for her to go home.

'The maxillofacial team want to see you again next Friday,' he told her, referring to the specialist surgeons who'd managed her facial injuries. Her face was still swollen, particularly around her eyes, and at a later date she might need another skin graft to the side of her neck, but things appeared to be improving daily.

'I hope to get your plaster off in another five weeks or so but in the meantime it's important that you keep up the walking. In about eighteen months we'll remove that nail we've put in your leg. That'll be a fairly minor procedure and nothing to worry about.'

'Thank you so much, Doctors.' Elaine Perry beamed at them. 'No offence, but I'd walk to Wales if it meant I could leave hospital. Not that it hasn't been very nice, having my meals cooked and everything, but you know how it is when you just want to be at home.'

'We'll see you in Fracture Clinic in two weeks,' Adam added, smiling. 'The ward clerk will give you your appointment.'

'We should be able to discharge the rest of that room by Christmas Eve,' he said to Christopher as they moved on to the last cubicle on Chamberlain Ward. 'Mrs Donald and Mr Reid and perhaps one or two of the others should be ready to go home by New Year's Eve, which means we'll be starting the year back to our normal bed numbers around here.'

'So it'll work out well if I'm away for the long week over New Year?'

Adam looked sharply at his registrar. 'Fine.' Because there was no elective surgery that week, it was the quietest time of the year and he was happy for his registrar to take time off, though, like Adam, Christopher rarely bothered to take the leave he was allocated. 'What are you planning?'

'Nina and I thought we'd go skiing in Austria.'

'Nina?' Adam frowned. 'What about Monica?'

He'd assumed the younger man was still besotted with the teacher Barbara had introduced him to at her dinner party, but Chris merely shrugged a casual shoulder.

'Monica's old news,' he said evenly. 'Some flash American banker with a Corvette answered her advertisement last week so that was the end of me. Nina works at the same school. She teaches maths. She's great.'

'Good. Good.' Adam slanted him a sideways look, envying Chris his nonchalance.

He reminded himself that at Chris's age he'd been just as casual about changing relationships. Only not now, he admitted, acknowledging that he was still stinging from the affair with Susan.

Affair was an exaggeration, he conceded. It would have been more accurate to say that he was still stinging from his *non*-affair with Susan. But then stinging was the problem. Because 'stinging' didn't convey any sense of nights spent pacing floors or distracted hours spent staring at the wall in his office, nor did it hint at the dull, cold, aching lump that had been sitting in the pit of his stomach since the morning he'd walked out of her flat.

He didn't kid himself that walking out had been his own idea. But she'd been right to send him away. Her tight little words before he'd left that morning had rammed the truth of his behaviour back into his face like a punching ball. He'd acted atrociously, he'd realised. He'd been intent on his own desires and careless of hers, smugly convinced that he'd known what was best for another human being. He'd been guilty of everything she'd accused him of and the recognition of how arrogantly he'd behaved towards her appalled him.

So he'd walked out that day then had left her alone. He'd not called her or tried to see her although he'd thought of little else. He'd noted the times she visited Tony and avoided being on Chamberlain then. He'd ignored the messages Annabel had left with his secretary because he'd known that communicating with her was simply another way in which they'd both tried to manipulate Susan into consenting to something she'd never wanted.

To face up to the truth about himself and his behaviour had been hard but he'd done it. It had been three weeks and it bothered him that he wasn't getting over her. Why, instead of a brief passing regret that things hadn't worked out and perhaps a little of the relief which had always accompanied the ending of his relationships, did he feel so…bereft? Why wasn't his life coming back to normal?

'Dale Simpson says she's happy to cover for that week,' Chris was saying. 'It shouldn't be too bad. We're on call the Monday and Thursday but both weekends are free.'

'Whatever.' Adam didn't mind what arrangements the two registrars came to. Dale, although his research registrar now, had worked for him for the six months prior to Chris's appointment and she was a hard-working and enthusiastic surgeon.

'Tony's CT scan from this morning should be back,' Chris said. They were at the main desk now and he crouched beside the X-ray trolley. He pushed the films up onto the board and Adam leaned closer.

'Good callus formation at the symphysis,' he noted, meaning that the fracture through the front of Tony's pelvis was healing. 'Some signs of improvement at the sacroiliac,' he added, referring to one of the joints at the back of his pelvis. He'd been concerned on the plain films that there hadn't been much healing activity—new, healing bone showed up whiter on the films—but the CT reassured him. 'Good. That's better than I'd hoped for. Another eight weeks and that should be strong.'

'I'll tell Dr Wheelan,' Chris said. 'She was asking me yesterday about his progress. She didn't seem to understand that three months is optimistic for posterior fractures. She thought that because we weren't taking him out yet and making him walk around things were bad.'

Adam noted his registrar's bewildered expression and the fact that Susan now communicated with Chris rather than him with a shrug. 'You'll find she hasn't the first clue about orthopaedics,' he remarked evenly, perturbed that that characteristic of hers seemed suddenly endearing. He remembered how on that first day he'd referred Tony to her she'd wanted him to take out his bolts and pins so she could transfer him to a psychiatric ward. At the time his response had been one of exasperated impatience but now the thought of her ludicrous order made him smile.

'Did you ask her about Tony's depression?' Tony's mood had unquestionably brightened over the last two weeks and he'd noticed that morning that there'd been no psychiatric nurse in attendance when Tony's bed had been wheeled past their round for his scan. 'Does she still consider him suicidal?'

'She was in a hurry and I didn't get to ask her anything,' Chris told him. 'Shall I call her this afternoon?'

'No, I'll talk to her.' It was business, he told himself. Nothing else. And it had been three weeks. What harm could it do?

'Four hundred and something toasters,' Susan said wearily. 'It's been a nightmare for all of us.'

She was in Duncan's office after their round on Winchester Ward and her colleague smiled at her sympathetically. 'But the stores must understand they have to take them back,' he countered. 'Can't one of the social workers simply telephone them?'

'The big stores we've contacted have all agreed. They've checked their delivery dockets to tell us how many they sold her and we're in the process of sending those back. But that still leaves more than two hundred which probably come from little shops, and as she's destroyed the receipts we've no idea which ones. The manufacturers won't take them back but some of them are looking up the batch numbers for us so we might be able to work out where they were sent from.'

'Is your patient any help?'

'She's too euphoric. All she can talk about is toasters and toast and making toast for the wedding. She doesn't want to help. In fact, she thinks they're terrific.'

'And in the meantime toasters keep arriving?'

'Part of the reason I admitted her was just to stop her accepting deliveries,' Susan admitted. 'Her social worker's put notices on her door to say no responsibility will be taken for any more but the odd box is still being left out back. At least that way they're still labelled and they can be sent back so it's not so bad. But, Duncan, you should see the house. When I went to see her it was toasters from ceiling to floor.'

'How much do you think she's spent?'

'Thousands.' Susan shook her head. 'She didn't have a lot of money to spare as it was.'

Lillian Brooks had been her patient for five years, but before that Susan's predecessor at St Martin's had looked after her for two decades. She couldn't tolerate lithium, the conventional treatment for manic depression, which normally kept people relatively stable, and the commonly used alternative of anticonvulsant medications had never been effective with her.

Because of that, Lillian's emotional see-sawing between manic and depressive episodes was nothing new, but Susan had never seen her so high before. A wedding invitation had prompted her to accumulate toasters, and she'd spent the previous month travelling all over London on her bus pass, buying and ordering dozens at a time.

'We'll get her calm again easily enough but that's when the trouble's really going to start,' Susan said worriedly. 'Unless we can get all the toasters returned and the money back, I'm frightened she'll take one look at a bank statement, realise what she's done, then see-saw straight into the sort of depression that could take months to lift again.'

'I could use a new toaster.' Duncan looked thoughtful. 'I'll buy one. And the staffroom needs a replacement. That's two.'

'I'm buying one and Rachel's getting one for Christmas,' Susan added, feeling herself beginning to smile a little. 'Plus Annabel's taking one and Mike's taking one for his work and I've managed to sell one to Chamberlain Ward where Tony Dundas is.'

Her bleep shrilled and she checked the number that came up on its side, reaching for Duncan's telephone and calling it automatically. 'But that's only six,' she continued to her colleague, while she waited for her call to be answered. 'Out of hundreds. I need to sell another thirty just to clear the ones I've carted up to my office. That's not much of a start—'

'Seven double six three.' He only said the number but although it was several weeks since they'd spoken she knew his voice immediately. 'Susan…?' When she still didn't say anything he repeated her name. 'Susan? Is that you?'

'It is.' She swallowed heavily, shaking her head at Duncan's silent miming about whether he should leave because that didn't seem fair since she was in his office. 'Yes. Yes, it is.'

'How's Tony?' He sounded brisk. 'He isn't being specialled today.'

'No, I've scaled down his supervision,' she said unevenly. 'From now on he'll be having an hour with a nurse every afternoon and I'm seeing him twice a week. He's doing well. Keeping the contact's still important, I think, but he's doing well in the family work and I'm confident he's no longer suicidal.'

She wasn't sure whether he was interested in what they'd achieved but it seemed a good, neutral subject to continue. 'We were right about the death of his mother being the cause of the family conflict,' she told him.

'The broken leg that led to her admission to hospital was caused by her slipping in oil that Tony had spilled. Mentally he took the blame for everything that happened after that and subconsciously his father blamed him as well. They've done fairly well in therapy. Tony and his father seem closer now. Um…it might speed things up if he could get about a bit more. Are you sure you can't take him out of that triangle thing sooner rather than later?'

He made a small sound that she thought might have been a sigh. 'I'm sure,' he said heavily. 'Twelve weeks at this stage is the minimum.'

'Yes, Christopher did say something about that,' she said vaguely, finding it difficult to concentrate when she had to put up with not just Adam being there on the other end of the line but Duncan performing a peculiar mime in front of her.

Adam was saying something in her ear about pelvic bones and how they healed but she was trying to understand the increasingly violent movements Duncan was making with his hands. It was only when he wrote a word followed by a large question mark on his jotting pad that she understood.

'Adam, do you need a toaster?' she asked weakly, not happy about forcing such a thing on him but not seeing that she had much choice. Her question drew an approving beam from Duncan, who slumped back into his chair with an air of mock exhaustion. 'We have some for sale.'

'Toasters?'

'Yes.'

She worried her lower lip between her teeth as his hesitation stretched, wanting to tell him that it didn't matter but fearing that it would only make her appear even more ludicrous to him than usual.

Finally he said, 'I could buy a toaster. OK, yes. How do you want to organise it? Shall I post you a cheque?'

'Made out to Lillian Brooks,' she told him. 'It might be easier to pay when you take delivery because that way I can tell you the definite price. Shall I bring one across to you or would you like to…come to the department to collect it?'

She caught a movement out of the corner of her eye and swung the chair around again in time to catch Duncan leaving.

When Adam didn't say anything immediately she rushed on, flushing at the thought that he might guess from her invitation how startlingly she'd found herself missing him these past three weeks, 'I ask because I've about three dozen in my office so if you came here you could choose the model you prefer.'

'There can't be that many differences between them,' he said. 'Just courier one across. I'll pick up the bill.'

'You'd be surprised by how many differences there are,' she insisted. 'I mean, do you want two slices or four?'

'Two.'

'Automatic or manual operation?'

'Manual.'

'Do you eat muffins?'

'Never.'

'Crumpets?'

'Susan—'

'What about one that chimes when it pops up?'

'Are you saying you want to see me?'

'I wouldn't want to pick the wrong toaster,' she said weakly.

'Susan, just—'

'Yes. Yes, I do,' she interjected, sure at least, after talking to him, of that. She couldn't go on like this. Not leaving things…unresolved. She didn't know what she was going to say to him or what she wanted to achieve from the meeting, outside of selling one more toaster, but, however pathetic it made her seem, she longed to see him. 'If you want. I'll be in my office from six…no, sorry, from seven.'

*   *   *

The lights of Adam's car came into sight as it rounded the sweeping drive leading to the psychiatric department at seven fifty-seven and twenty-five seconds.

Susan knew when he came because she'd been standing at her window, waiting, for almost an hour and she knew the time exactly because the digital alarm on her desk had been a Christmas gift from Duncan the year before and it had come with a guarantee to remain accurate into the next century.

She met him on the ground floor, opening the building's door using her security card from the inside so he wouldn't have to walk around through one of the wards.

He was wearing a dark suit and tie with a white shirt and he looked strong and powerful and utterly magnificent, but as he strode into the reflected light of the building he saw that his expression was remote and his regard, as it rested on her face, unreadable.

She swallowed, amazing herself with the thought that this man had once slept almost naked against her. 'Hi.'

'Hi.'

The formalities over, she lowered her gaze as he came into the building, then carefully pulled the glass doors shut. 'It's a security thing, not being able to get in here at night,' she explained huskily, leading the way to the stairs. 'Cameras monitor the ward entrances and there're intercoms there so going via a ward's the only way to come through.'

He didn't say anything and she felt herself growing even more stiff and awkward as she led him up to her office.

'Toasters,' she said huskily, sweeping her arm to indicate the array she'd prepared. 'I've stacked them in alphabetical order by brand.' She faltered a little at the look he sent her then, but as it was no more readable than the one he'd given her downstairs she forced herself to go on. 'I forgot to ask if you preferred stainless steel or coloured, but there're some of each there.'

He picked up the nearest one. 'This is fine.'

'It's a four-slice one.'

'Four's fine.'

'You said you preferred two.'

'I'll take four.' Putting it on her desk, he took a cheque book out of the pocket of his jacket. 'How much?'

Mrs Brooks's social worker had obtained price lists from the manufacturers and Susan checked his against them. 'Thirty-nine pounds, please. To L. M. Brooks.'

She waited for him to finish writing it out but his pen didn't move. 'Are you trying to sell all of these?'

'More if I can,' she admitted. 'One of my patients...well it's a long story.'

'Give me six.'

She blinked. 'Adam, that's not necessary.'

'It's almost Christmas. I'll give them away.' Not giving her any time to argue, he wrote a sum on the cheque and signed it. 'Two thirty-four pounds,' he said, passing it to her as if he thought she might want to check the sum. She looked at it automatically, although she had no idea if it was right because such an effort of mathematics seemed completely beyond her at that moment.

'Thank you.'

It came out like a little husky croak but he didn't seem to notice. 'Thank you for supplying the toasters,' he said evenly.

'I'm very grateful—'

'Don't be.' His mouth tightened and he lifted one hand sharply to cut her off. 'You don't have to be, Susan. I'm not trying to make you feel grateful. It was an equal transaction. I...needed a toaster. Toasters. And you simply supplied them.'

'But six…?' Despite the tension which had had her stomach surging all afternoon since she'd spoken to him, she felt the corners of her mouth lift at that. 'Adam, you can't possibly need six.'

'You're laughing at me.'

'I'm not,' she protested, but, happy as she was to have cleared some of her toaster collection, she couldn't help herself. The thought of six of Mrs Brooks's toasters sitting gift-wrapped around his Christmas tree seemed suddenly hilarious.

She turned away and walked swiftly to the window, but he must have seen her shoulders shaking because he came after her.

'What have I done that's so funny?'

'I don't know,' she managed between silent chuckles, squeezing her eyes shut and turning her head to avoid seeing his startled face because that only made it seem more funny.

'Are you hysterical?'

She shook harder. 'I…think…I might be,' she whispered between gasps. She wondered if his guests would be puzzled by how similar their presents looked in their wrappings. She wondered if there'd be a lot of pre-Christmas speculation about what the gifts contained. She pictured Lawrence's reaction to the gift of a toaster and that made her laughter deepen.

'Should I slap you?'

'No!' She almost squealed when he looked serious. 'No.'

'Susan?' She saw that he looked genuinely worried now but she still couldn't control herself. Overcoming her puny efforts to twist her head away, he took her cheeks between his hands and tilted her face up to his. He took away her glasses then wiped at her damp cheeks with the pads of his thumbs. 'Susan? Are you all right?'

She tried to say that she was fine, that this would pass, that she could even feel her hysteria starting to ebb in the full, overwhelming awareness of the closeness of his body, that everything would be all right if he just…kissed her, but before she could form the words that was exactly what he was doing and it was wonderful.

She calmed, opening her mouth as soon as he touched her, abruptly hungry for him. But instead of the passionate embrace she craved, after that first, glorious kiss his hands went to her hips and although she could feel the warmth of him through her jeans he held her away from him while he took only quick, short, frustrating bites at her mouth.

'I don't want to do this,' he muttered harshly, between nips. 'Stop me.'

'I don't want you to stop.' Linking her hands around his neck, she tried to push herself against him, tried to make him hold her properly. But the hands at her hips kept her firmly away. 'Kiss me properly,' she whispered. 'Please.'

'Don't do this, Susan.' It was almost a groan. His mouth moved over hers to cover it completely. 'Stop playing games. I wasn't pretending. I won't be able to stop.'

'Then make love to me.' She touched his mouth greedily, dizzy, lost. She hadn't touched alcohol yet she felt the way she imagined it felt to be drunk.

His hands slid from her hips to her buttocks, curled under her, squeezed her, then bounced her hard against him. 'Feel what you're doing to me,' he ordered hoarsely. 'Feel what you always do to me. Now do you understand what I'm saying?'

'I understand and I like it,' she whispered urgently. She

didn't know how else to convince him that she wanted him. 'Please, Adam. Stop teasing me.'

'Stop *teasing you*?' With a harshly muttered word that left her momentarily shocked, he twisted away from her, putting the width of her desk between them. 'Stop there, Susan,' he warned when she started towards him. 'Talk. Talk fast.'

She retrieved her glasses from her desk where he'd left them and pushed them on, wanting to see him properly. 'You were right,' she said breathlessly. 'You were right that it was silly for me to sit around, waiting for ever for the perfect man. Annabel's right when she says that life has to be lived. I've spent all my life being cautious and it hasn't made me happy. But you do. Deliriously. When I'm with you the world melts away. You're very…sexy. No other man has ever made me feel the way I do with you. I'd be crazy not to have sex with you.'

'Three weeks ago you sent me away for saying that.'

'I felt as if you were sweeping me off my feet. I'm not like you or Annabel. I don't make decisions like click, click, click.' She snapped her fingers to show what she meant. 'I do things slowly. I think about everything. The way you were…was too rushed for me. I felt pushed. I felt as if I was being forced into something I hadn't decided that I wanted. I needed time to work out what my own feelings were. I needed space. I didn't mean for you to go away for ever.'

'Now you've decided you want sex with me?'

'If the option's still there,' she said nervously. When he'd left that day and not contacted her again she'd thought it had been taken away from her, but the way he'd responded tonight had made her hopeful again. 'Now I've thought about it more. Yes.'

'Coolly and calmly, you've decided you want to have sex with me.'

'Yes.' She nodded.

'Away from the heat of the moment, no passion involved, you've decided that the right time has come for you to make love.'

'That's right.'

'You've waited thirty-four years for your perfect man but now you've decided that you might as well grab something anyway because Mr Wonderful just might not turn up.'

'Not thirty-four years,' she said automatically, rubbing at her arms as her nervousness started increasing again. 'I wasn't waiting for him when I was a child. Ten years,' she conceded. 'Fifteen, perhaps. Actually, I wasn't really even waiting for anybody—'

'No dice, Susan.'

She'd had a shivery premonition in those last moments but still it shocked her. 'B-but just before—'

'You're not using me like that.'

'It's not using you,' she protested. 'And it's what you wanted. Three weeks ago you couldn't keep your hands off—'

'Three weeks ago I didn't realise I'd fallen in love with the most infuriating woman in London,' he countered harshly.

He looked, she realised, almost as shocked as she was by the declaration. But he recovered faster. While she stood, still numb and speechless, he retrieved the first toaster he'd chosen. 'Courier the others to my office,' he said thickly, stalking away from her.

'By the way, you *can* have me, Susan.' He'd turned, as if struck by an afterthought, in her doorway. 'But I want a wedding band first. There's no rush. Unless you're des-

perate, of course. I'm not going to push you or manipulate
you. I'm going to let you decide what's best for you. Think
about it for as long as you like. If I get a better offer in
the meantime I'll let you know.'

It took her about four minutes to make up her mind but
by that time his car was gone. 'Four minutes, Susan,' she
murmured, going for the telephone. 'Four minutes for the
most important decision of your life? You're a changed
woman.'

But the telephonists on duty refused to give her Adam's
address. 'It's against all the rules, Dr Wheelan,' the second
one she tried insisted. 'I can only page him for you but as
he's not on call he won't be wearing his bleep.'

Susan rang Trauma and Churchill and Chamberlain but
the nurses on each claimed the same. Finally, knowing she
had no choice, she called Annabel.

'Adam's address or Barbara's telephone number, please.
Whatever you've got and no questions,' she said tightly,
when her sister answered.

To her surprise, perhaps as startled at Susan's firm tone
as Susan was herself, Annabel gave her Barbara's number
uncomplainingly. But she spoiled it by throwing in a quick
question. 'By any chance, should I be buying myself a
posh hat?'

'I'll tell you tomorrow.' Wincing at her squeal, Susan
cut her off and called Barbara.

Lawrence answered brightly and gave her the information she wanted without hesitation. 'Just never tell Barbara
I told you,' he muttered. 'She'd kill me. She's still trying
to talk him into meeting some ballet dancer she's found.'

A ballet dancer? Realising that in any contest with a
ballet dancer a dithering psychiatrist would only come off
second best, Susan thought it best to hurry.

Beyond registering that his home was an attractive

house in a leafy street in Highgate, Susan only noticed that his car was there and that there were lights on.

'Marry me,' she gasped, when he opened the door. 'Please.'

He took her shaking hands and tugged her inside, closed the door then pressed her back against it, his hands either side of her head. 'Because you're desperate for my body?'

'Because I love you.'

He smiled at her and it felt like the most wonderful thing she'd ever seen. 'Because I'm Mr Perfect.'

'Because you're arrogant and smug and pushy,' she whispered. 'Because I don't understand a word you're saying when you talk about your work but I still love to listen to you. Because I haven't been able to think of anything but you since you tried to undress me in that pub the first night. You're not Mr Perfect but I'm not looking for him any more because I'm in love with you. Am I allowed to have sex now?'

'When you've put a wedding band here.' Laughingly fending off her attempts to embrace him, he held out the third finger of his left hand. 'Not before, you terrible hussy.'

'Just sleep with me, then.'

'No. I don't trust you.' Still laughing, he covered her indignant face with tiny kisses. 'Now walk up the stairs,' he told her huskily. 'I want to watch your bottom.'

'I put them on especially for you,' she confessed, twirling. She'd changed their appointment from six until seven that evening to give herself time to go home and change out of the suit she'd been wearing for work. 'I thought you hadn't noticed.'

'You knew I'd noticed.' His thumbs brushed the tight buttons of the nipples her T-shirt outlined. 'Immediately. But until the wedding I want you in suits.' His eyes on her breasts, he slid his hands up and gently plumped them together. 'And jackets,' he said huskily. 'Thick, bulky jackets.'

'And after?' she demanded, spellbound by the soft, rolling movements of his hands.

'Pink bikini bottoms,' he said hoarsely. 'And whatever you were wearing under your coat that day I came for breakfast.'

They paid extra for a special licence so they could marry on Christmas Eve. 'Because there's no elective orthopaedic surgery between Christmas and New Year,' Susan explained to everyone who asked, keeping her own reasons for their urgency private. 'It's the only time it's easy for Adam to take leave.'

Neither of them wanted a big performance and they had a small gathering of friends and relatives in the hospital chapel. Afterwards their guests came back with them to the house for the champagne and luncheon Barbara and Annabel had organised.

Everyone except Adam and Susan drank far too much, and when Annabel cornered Susan in the bedroom just as she was preparing to leave the thickness of her perfume barely masked the champagne fumes.

'Just one thing, Susie,' she warbled. 'You've got to tell me. After all these years, how was it?'

Susan smiled. 'Ask me after the honeymoon,' she said warmly. She kissed Annabel's cheek. 'Thank you. Goodbye.'

Everyone gathered downstairs to see them off. After the hugs and kisses, just as they were turning away, Susan's arm entwined with her husband's, she thought she heard Annabel utter the word 'virgin'.

When it was followed by a disbelieving shriek from

Barbara, Susan turned around sharply, but both women beamed back at her so innocently that she decided she was probably being overly paranoid.

Adam opened the door. 'Ready, my darling?'

Susan looked at his tin-canned car and Lawrence's proud expression as he stood waiting beside it and sighed. She'd packed Annabel's pink bikini along with the thick old flannelette nightie she'd been too embarrassed to let him see at her flat that day, plus her toothbrush and strawberry lip gloss. She couldn't think of another thing she could possibly need. 'Ready, my darling.'

Two nights after their return from Paris Susan turned on the television for the first time in ten days, deciding it was time she took an interest in something other than her new husband's body. A news item was on, a report about the inquiry into the M1 coach crash, and the caption under the interviewee's name made her freeze.

The instant it was over she dashed back up to the bedroom. 'You were just on the BBC,' she cried, trying not to be distracted by the breadth of Adam's naked chest as he sprawled on their bed, reading. It had been an old report, showing him giving the casualty numbers on the night of the crash. 'You've never told me you're an associate professor of surgery!'

'I'm not.' Adam looked at her over his journal. 'Since December the second I've been a professor of surgery.'

'You rat!' She thrust a pillow at his laughing face. 'Why didn't you tell me?

'I was worried you'd think I was too intellectual,' he murmured, gathering her into his arms then tumbling her over into the covers. 'Secretly it turned you on, thinking I was dim and controllable.'

'I'm turned on now,' she whispered, parting her legs so

that he could sink between them. 'And you've never been controllable.'

'I adore you.'

'I love you.' She arched her body, welcoming his embrace. 'My brainy professor.'

MILLS & BOON®

Makes any time special

Enjoy a romantic novel from
Mills & Boon®

Presents™ Enchanted™ Temptation®

Historical Romance™ Medical Romance™

COMING NEXT MONTH from 6th August

ONE IN A MILLION by Margaret Barker
Bundles of Joy

Sister Tessa Grainger remembered Max Forster when he arrived as consultant on her Obs and Gynae ward, for she'd babysat when his daughter Francesca was small. But Max wasn't the carefree man she'd known. Tessa wanted him to laugh again and—maybe—even love again…

POLICE SURGEON by Abigail Gordon

Dr Marcus Owen was happy to be a GP and Police Surgeon, until he found one of the practice partners was Caroline Croft, the woman he'd once loved. Caroline was equally dismayed, for she still loved Marcus! Brought back together by their children, where did they go from here?

IZZIE'S CHOICE by Maggie Kingsley

Sister Isabella Clark came back to discover a new broom A&E consultant, but being followed around by Ben Farrell ended with her speaking her mind and Ben apologised! Since he liked her "honesty", Izzie kept it up, but it wasn't until the hospital fête that they realised they might have something more…

THE HUSBAND SHE NEEDS by Jennifer Taylor
A Country Practice #4

When District Nurse Abbie Fraser hears that Nick Delaney is home, she isn't sure how she feels, for Nick is now in a wheelchair. Surely she can make Nick see he has a future? But at what cost to herself, when she realises she has never stopped loving him?

Available at most branches of WH Smith, Tesco, Asda, Martins, Borders, Easons, Volume One/James Thin and most good paperback bookshops

THE

Regency

COLLECTION

Where rogues find romance

Look out for the fourth volume in this limited collection of Regency Romances from Mills & Boon® in August.

Featuring:

The Outrageous Dowager
by Sarah Westleigh

and

Devil-May-Dare
by Mary Nichols

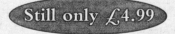

Still only £4.99

MILLS & BOON®

Makes any time special™

Available at most branches of WH Smith, Tesco, Martins, Borders, Easons, Volume One/James Thin and most good paperback bookshops

2 FREE

books and a surprise gift!

We would like to take this opportunity to thank you for reading this Mills & Boon® book by offering you the chance to take TWO more specially selected titles from the Medical Romance™ series absolutely FREE! We're also making this offer to introduce you to the benefits of the Reader Service™—

* ★ FREE home delivery
* ★ FREE gifts and competitions
* ★ FREE monthly Newsletter
* ★ Exclusive Reader Service discounts
* ★ Books available before they're in the shops

Accepting these FREE books and gift places you under no obligation to buy, you may cancel at any time, even after receiving your free shipment. Simply complete your details below and return the entire page to the address below. *You don't even need a stamp!*

YES! Please send me 2 free Medical Romance books and a surprise gift. I understand that unless you hear from me, I will receive 4 superb new titles every month for just £2.40 each, postage and packing free. I am under no obligation to purchase any books and may cancel my subscription at any time. The free books and gift will be mine to keep in any case.

M9EA

Ms/Mrs/Miss/Mr ....Initials...................................
                                                                BLOCK CAPITALS PLEASE

Surname ....

Address ....

....

....Postcode...................................

Send this whole page to:
THE READER SERVICE, FREEPOST CN81, CROYDON, CR9 3WZ
(Eire readers please send coupon to: P.O. BOX 4546, DUBLIN 24.)